The Land of
Somewhere Safe

NewCon Press Novellas

The Land of Somewhere Safe

Hal Duncan

NewCon Press
England

First published in the UK by NewCon Press
41 Wheatsheaf Road, Alconbury Weston, Cambs, PE28 4LF
September 2018

NCP 165 (limited edition hardback)
NCP 166 (softback)

10 9 8 7 6 5 4 3 2 1

ISBN:

978-1-910935-89-7 (hardback)
978-1-910935-90-3 (softback)

Cover art by Ben Baldwin
Cover layout by Ian Whates

Minor Editorial meddling by Ian Whates
Book layout by Storm Constantine

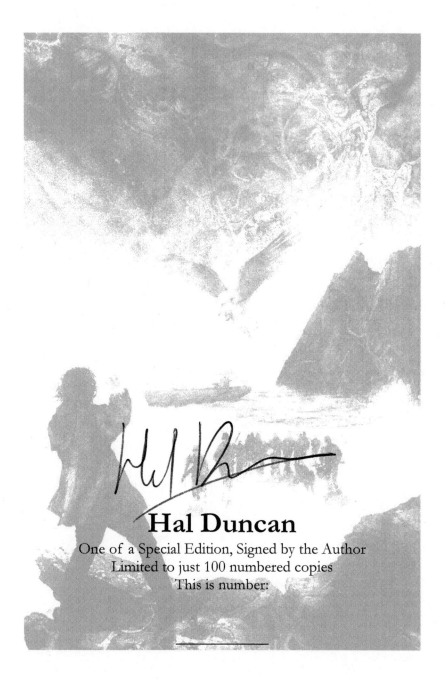

Hal Duncan

One of a Special Edition, Signed by the Author
Limited to just 100 numbered copies
This is number:

_____

For Jack and Jaimee.

Part One

• 1

– Will we be safe here? says the scamp.

Slickspit Hamshankery, prentice fabbler, scruffles the nipper's hair and tussles her into a hug – *Don't be daft, of course it's safe* – but his glance away has its own worry in it, eyes looking to his mentor for assurance. At the covered window, in the gloom, Gobfabbler Halyard-Dunkling, Esquire, turns from taping one last black bin bag into place, looks pointedly round at the gaggle of shivering scamps lit by mobile phones.

– Now, Slick, he says. Don't you be filling them nippers' noggins with piffle. Does this feel bleedin safe to you?

The lounge in this gutted cottage is a hollow of rotting floorboards and mould, grim as the moor Flashjack floored the minibus through to get here, dismal as the weather and looming hills, the desolate building with *Jimmy the Beast* spraypainted on one wall, visible from the winding road the scallywag stopped on only long enough for them to pile out, leg it round back: one scallywag, Quippersnap Rannigant, crowbar in hand to prise the board from a window; two scrags, Slickspit and Gobfabbler; someteen rucksacked scamps that they puntied in through broken glass, and followed.

– I'll give yer *safe*.

He knew it wouldn't be safe, just as Quip did, when the two of them decided to take Gob's offer, to take the Stamp. They were warned. It might be safer for two runaways than today's London streets, and for sure it's safer being a Scruffian *now*, Gob'd said, than back when *he* had no choice about it. And having your soul, every intricacy of your essence, read and written in black on your chest, fixed forever and yourself Fixed with it... did have its perks. So said the imperishable urchin from before Queen Victoria. There'd been disappearances though. Raids.

– But it's maybes safe enough *for now*, says Gob. Quip?

At the hall doorway, sortie over, Quippersnap nods: *secure*. Noggins turn from scallywag to scrag, peepers wide for cues from their biggers. Slick points the scamp in his arm at a rucksack: *get your sleeping bag and – that's it*. As Gob settles himself to cross-legged before them, the scamps have their cue.

– That's right, says Gob. Blankies round yer. Cosy up. We can't have a fire, but if yer all snuggles tight, maybes I can fabble yer summat to get us through the cold night, eh?

And he begins:

• 2

See, as even yer icklest scamp or scrag will tell yer, as even yer daftest scallywag or scofflaw knows, ain't nowheres in this world *truly* safe for any waif, least of all us Scruffians what any groanhuff as knows of would scrub in a jiffy. Why, if the Stamp hadn't been secret, if the Trade weren't off the books, oh, if they hadn't swept our whole history under the rug for shame after we nicked that Stamp and burnt their bleeding Institute to ash, they'd be Fixing and selling waifs to this day, nippers. You *mind* how it were, eh?

Safe? Fuck safe! Weren't safe for Flashjack back in Georgy Porgy's day, when he were tarting his fizzog for nonce's fists down Moorfields molly market, thruppence for a thump. Weren't safe for Puckerscruff plying the same rough trade when he weren't even Fixed yet, taking punter's slaps and stranglings, and him not springing back licketysplit like us. Weren't safe for Foxtrot back *forever* ago, when's he hadn't yet tweaked his Stamp to sproing his cunt to a cock, so's every miller or cobbler as owned him down the centuries, they'd say he *was too* a girl, and sod the truth!

Weren't safe for *you* scruffs, was it? Even you what's joined us since, took the Stamp yerselves, Fixed by choice – maybe yer ain't had the chains and chimneys and losing yer right foot to the mills five bleedin weeks in a row, but *you* ain't here cause yer foster home was peachy, eh, Quippersnap? And maybe them stickmen ain't around to scrobble and scrub us now, but of all us here, nippers, clear as the freckles Fixed in a squiggle, ain't none of yer peepers don't veritably *projectify* the savvy that *it ain't never safe nowheres*.

In *this* world anyways.

See, you all's heard the fabble of the Land of Nod, ain't yer? Where's Keen ended up after scrubbing Able... as the groanhuffs' Holy Bollocks has it leastways. And yer knows the *truth* of that lie, eh, how *both* brothers scarpered to that dreamland, how Keen didn't *really* scrub his brother's Stamp, just tweaked it summat *wild*. Like as an urchin might tweak himself knucklespikes, Keen rewrote Able *out of reality*, into this hideyhole playground. And went in after him, to the land where every scruff plays safely now in their sleep.

But that ain't *real*, yer says?

Think again.

• 3

Don't you listen to them streak-of-piss scofflaws what says it's just a fib for the scamps, bedtime bollocks so's the brats won't wake in a wet bed, screaming for a mam two centuries dead, dreaming they's back in the Institute, getting their soul ripped out and wrote on their chest all over again. Some scofflaw cocks their snoot, sneers as how *of course* them littl'uns is *Fixed* in that moment so they *blah blah blah*...? You just tell em that's what tweaking's for – to *snip* such fears – so shut the fuck up.

No. It ain't *just a fabble*.

Oh, it's a wonderland, it is, scamps, *every* wonderland. The Land of Nod, we calls it when we fabbles Keen and Able, but just as Keen and Able, being veritable Scruffian *gods*, has other monickers, just as sometimes we calls them brothers Dinguses and Apple, or Baccy and Pillow, well, sometimes we calls that place Appleland or Turn-an-Knock or Mug Mall or Cuckooine. There's so many fabbles of it, even the groanhuffs has names for it.

But one name they'd never think to call it, but you *might* have heard it called, is the Land of Somewhere Safe.

See, that's where all em whatsits and whodjamaflips goes when yer says to yerself, *I must put this Somewhere Safe*. And then yer goes to get it, and it ain't where yer thunk it was, and yer ain't sure if yer just forgot where the fuck yer cunning hidey was – *too* fucking cunning, it was. Well, that's Dinguses snaffling yer dinguses away in answer to yer wishes. He's only taken it to the

Land of Somewhere Safe for yer, innit!
And you know how come we knows that's true?
Because it ain't only in dreams *some* Scruffians have been there.

See, it were during the Blitz, scamps, back when the doodlebugs was falling, and the East End being flattened, and one dark night, all the crib bosses from all across London was parlaying in Squirlet's den, to conflab on how's to keep the Stamp safe, and Foxtrot pipes up...
– Gentlemen, says he, ladies, please!
Cause they's all babbling over each other, being Scruffians, and them as was bosses just the least bossable of the unbossable, really.
– If we need to put it somewhere safe, says Foxtrot, we need to put it *Somewhere Safe.*
And that night... a Plan were hatched.

• 4

1939 it were, and a dark time in London. Why, the goanhuffs had stockpiled coffins, circled the city with barrage balloons against the Zeppelins, even drawn up plans to evacuate all the kiddiwinks from the city. So when the war begun with the Blitz, a full fifty-seven days of doodlebugs dropping, and the East End them Nazis' Target A –
No, it were 1939, Slick, cause the Yanks hadn't joined yet.
No, they *was too* doodlebugs.
I don't care what Wikipedia says. They must've had em, else how could they have the Blitz?
Well, the *evacuation* must've been 1940 then.

So. When it were safe enough to come out of the shelters, them groanhuffs thinks to themselves, right ho, time to put their plan into action. Operation Pied Piper it were called. *Eight hundred thousand* nippers assembled at school gates and marched to train stations. Picture em, scamps! Luggage tags on lapels, gas masks in little box satchels, ration books in pockets, each humphing a suitcase and a brown paper bag with a tin of corned beef and buns, and all singing *Wish Me Luck As You Wave Me Goodbye*, like as they was going on a grand adventure. Blimey!

Now amongst all the kerfuffle of kiddiewinks at King's Cross, scamps, there was two as didn't know they acktcherly *was* in for a grand adventure. Peter Dearest and Lily Love we'll calls em, cause that's how they was called respectively by his doting mum and her proud father, right up until the sunny September Sunday when's they both, by unhappy not-so-accident, lost the one parent they'd left to the bombs what independently blasted to smithereens Peter's nice terraced redbrick on Earl's Court Square and Lily's lovely Georgian Chelsea townhouse. And their whole world with it, the poor orphans.

Weren't much they had in common beyond that, Lily and Peter, truth be told, cause for all's they was both of that middling well-to-do hoity-poloity world of *larders* and *dinner* – never *tea*, how common! – she were the posher but like to see snoots cocked at her, while he were of humbler roots but prone to cock his snoot. Cause Lily's long-lost mum were the brown Bombay bride of one of yer British Raj's finest, while Peter's yonks-popped dad were a grocer made good, so there was a fair old whack of... *attitudinal distinction*, let's say.

• 5

If any scruff had been there to see them two orphans then, on that cold December day, so early in the morning it was still pitch black, if any Scruffian had been slipping through the crowds to swipe a ticker here, a leather there, or idling against a wall, say, and seen them two, as they doddered their way along the platform, deep in a mob of bairns and brats and still being jounced by the groanhuffs jostling through... well, they might have been forgiven for pegging Peter as a twerp and Lily as a stray straight off the bat.

And that scruff wouldn't have been wholly wrong, scamps, cause that Lily could be a right tiger; she'd seen more'n her fair share of snootcocking at her swarth... and at the *punching* of cocked snoots... by a girl! Yeah, she'd a scamp's spirit, that tomboy tyke. But Peter, meanwhile, he were summat of a mouse, in truth, but if he sniffed a bit priggish at times... well, see, before yer *scallywag's* gangly limbs and hormones befuddles em, yer *scrag's* often sharper to what ain't safe and what ain't fair, and pricklier with it. And that's the age Peter were at.

Not that them two knowed scamps from scrags, or the strays what's just waiting for the Stamp from the twerps what's already a groanhuff cuntfucker inside. They hadn't even *heard* of Scruffians, them kids. It were decades since we sank the last Waifaker General in the Thames, mind. Weren't but a few unsprung scruffs by then, tucked away in the servants' wings of yer stateliest homes, so yer had to be of a *certain set* to know what's what. If they'd been Peter or Lily Fitzbastard-Fauntleroy-Smythe of Windsor, that'd be a whole other fabble. But they wasn't, mate.

So Lily wouln't never notice some kitchen skivvy as looked oddly familiar and familiarly odd, never click how the oddness was that scrag *staying* a scrag as Lily sprouted. Peter wouldn't never go off to school to the sight of a scallywag stableboy, and come back a decade later, as some pigfucking posh nob expelled from Eton in disgrace, to the exact same sight. So, as they passes that idling's scruff's lookout post, when Peter spots the graffiti – Chad peeping over a wall, long schnozz hanging down, *Wot, no Scruffians?* chalked above – he just wonders whatever on Earth *that* means.

• 6

So, barked aboard by groanhuffs with clipboards and clipped tones, flapped along the corridor by a flustery teacher, Miss Jessel – who's to accompany them, ensuring their *educative edification irregardless of evacuation, dear children* – Lily and Peter finds themselves sardined into a train compartment, into the stramash of four other kids and Miss Jessel, all inching, pivoting and elbowy – *excuse me; sorry; mind yer bonce; I do apologise* – passing luggage every which way, to jam – *here's a space for yer; oh, thanks ever so much* – the baggage rail full, until finally – *whew!* – they can all plonk down in the nearest seat.

In this train compartment then, as outside a porter rings a bell – *All aboard for Edinburgh! East Coast Main Line! Peterborough and Doncaster! York, Darlington and Durham! Newcastle, Berwick-Upon-Tweed and Edinburgh Waverley!* – here's Peter and Lily sat to the window side of Miss Jessel, looking across at two boys and two girls covering yer full range of scamp, scrag, scallywag and scofflaw, all in greatcoats and scarfs, schoolcaps and tanktops for the boys, cardigans and berets for the girls, looking *almost* as unremarkable as Peter and Lily themselves, but somehow managing to make that *almost* all that matters.

See, eldest to icklest, the littl'un interduces em, respectively: Janie; Jack; Sylvia; and himself being Kit – *at your service.* Bastable, their name is, says he, why, their grandfather's only Bastable of Arabia himself, disappeared in the Great War, alas, and their old man off now fighting in his father's bootsteps. And maybe it's the black hair curtaining quiet Janie's face, or the pencil 'tache drawn on ickle Kit's, both of which might be more at home in some Addams Family New Yorker cartoon our two hasn't even heard of, but the impression what they gives is... well, definitely somewhat *eccentric.*

Now Lily ain't fussed. Being a tyke like Kit and tomboy to boot, that 'tache just tickles her as admirably willful, no more untoward than herself fancying stetson and sixguns over golliwogs and wendy houses. But Peter, he's quite perturbed by these Bastables; why, both boys may be ginger, but Kit's napper is dapper as his genteel *Pleasure to meet you, dear chap*, while's Jack's scruffy shock's uncouth as his *Wotcha, mate!* Sylvia with her brusque *Hello* has a hint of Lily's brown to her, while silent Janie's pale as a ghost. Peter wouldn't hardly think em siblings at all!

• 7

All the long way to Waverley on the Flying Scotsman, Peter finds it curioser and curiouser. Them Bastables all conks out like tommies in the trenches used to snatching kip through the shortest second's peace; Miss Jessel is busying out the carriage as often as in, muttering about how they oughtn't be bound so far as *Edinburgh*; and Lily just buries her nose in a cowboy book; but Peter barely opens his American magazine with the spaceman on its cover, just gazes out the window at the countryside and stations slipping by, the skimmering of snow, all the while... wondering.

It gets curiouser still when, at Waverley, an *'undred* hours later, Waverley *at last*, they disembarks only for Miss Jessel to be hailed by a telegram boy: why, there's been a mix-up; they's to go to *Glasgow* now. Not *another* train! And in Glasgow, *there* she gets called to a telephone by a porter, comes back saying that ain't right neither. Further north they're bound, Fort bleeding William. And long past luncheon with packed lunches all eaten, Peter's famished now, so when's he rumpages in his pocket for money for a bun, what he finds is the purple pim!

– I've been pickpocketed! he bleats.

– I'll lend you some tin, pipes up Lily aside him, but then: Oh! Me too!

– Bugger, says a voice behind em: Jack, stood there in his plus fours and argylle socks, (him having outsprouted yer knee socks and school shorts of Peter and Kit, see,) Jack lighting a cigarette with a fingersnap, and puffing the flame out... only... Peter don't see him pocket the lighter. Odd. But then Miss Jessel's bundling em all on that Fort William train, and her fashing and flapping steamrollers all their laments, and it's onward, onward, *tssschtycoo! tssschtycoo! whoooo-whooooo!*

By the time they's on *another* steam train from Fort William, chuffing over the Glenfinnan Viaduct in the gloaming, through the gloomiest hills and glens, why, Peter's so hungry and tired, he couldn't say if he's coming or going, and he just wants to cry, just wants the mum he's trying ever so hard not to think of, wibbly lipped. By the time they's off that train and on the ferry crossing from Mallaig to Armadale, with the mist and dark descending,

he's so discombobblated and disconsolatrated, he don't even notice till Lily says it:
— Wherever has Miss Jessel gone?

• 8

Now Lily's made of sterner stuff, takes after her soldier Papa, so it's a bristly British *harrumph!* she gives when it turns out all the clipboard precision of yer evacuation operation at *one* end ain't been followed through in arranging *actual homes for em* at the other. It's a *Well, I never!* she mulligrumphs when the six kids is led into a town hall barely more'n a big wooden hut and *lined up on a stage* for groanhuffs to hem and haw over, gibbering in that inscrutable lilty singsong they calls the Gaelic. She's near boiling point, volcanic eruption, when —

CRACKOOM! The door of the hut's whipped smack into the wooden wall by a rising wind what whistles in now around the dark shape striding a grand entrance, all black furs and crow-feather boa, bobbed hair and cigarette holder. Scarlet liptick and emerald eyes. Leather driving gloves peeled off as she sweeps down the line: this way; whirl; that way; twirl. Why, it's Clan Chief Lady Morag Anne Fay MacGuffin, scamps, of Dunstravaigin Castle.
— I'll take that laddie! she says in lilty English. That lass! And those two! Och, all of them, blast it! I'll take all of them!

Well now, Lily looks to them other nippers, wide-eyed and gawping, cause she ain't sure if she's terrified of some wicked witch or enraptured by an idol of indomitable spirit, but all em others has multiplicitous looks: Peter petrified; Kit intrigued; Sylvia appreciative; Jack grinning blithely; Janie... well, invisible beneath that hair. And whichever way her own awe ought to fall, ain't nuffink to be done but go with the flow, which is a huchling out the door, lumbersome with baggage — *come now, chop chop!* — to the beautiful sleek black panther of a 1939 Bentley parked waiting for them.

— Och, ye've a sair stretch to see ye haim, Lady Fay, says the beardy Highlander what helps them stow some luggage in the boot, piles the rest atop the squeeze of em in each other's laps inside.
— Poppycock, Hector! says Lady Fay. We'll be home for supper. Modernity! Age of the automotive! We'll fly, mon, fly!
And fly they do, scamps. With a pinch of snuff from a little tin box and an *Onward, ho!* they's roaring off into the night, bounced this way and that by such twisty turns but so smooth the supension, they might almost *be* flying.

• 9

Well, that weaving as swayed em squidgy over each other leftward and rightwise must've been as a cradle's rocking, and the flashing flicker of headlights catching the twigs of barren tree branches whizzing by must've been veritably *hypnotic*, and the blankety ensconcing of thick mist and snug warmth inside the car must've been ever so cosying, cause it could only be that at some point in their hurtling along the unlit roads, each of them nippers nodded off. It could only be that. Cause suddenly they's all ablinky, juddering at a bump and braking.

 – Home at last! says Lady Fay.

And it's in they go, with baggage seeming made of lead now, so weary they all is at the end of that interminable journey. In they go, to a castle what's just a looming blackness in yer Stygian mist outside, but oh, which is as couthy as it's grand inside, with darkwood stairs so broad they can all walk up in a row, and – *oooooh!* – nosey down on em from the balcony around, before being huchled along up more steps, and another flight, and along a corridor, to finally unlumber in one room for the boys, one for the girls.

There's a dining room after that, a feast of venison stew they ravishes, Lily scarce noticing Jack Bastable's unseemly table manners. There's a drawing room with a grand piano and sofas, where's Lady Fay has em interduce emselves while sipping their choice of Horlicks, Ovaltine or Bovril. But she's gladdest, Lily is, of that bedroom, when they's back there, with hot water bottles for the beds, so blissfully unwindy as she unpacks her togs into her drawers, she scarce notices Janie clambering a dresser to pop a matchbox open, let a spider tippytoe out into a corner of the ceiling.

Peter weren't half so blithe, meanwhile, in the boy's room, as he folded his tanktop, placed it daintily upon a chair. Undid his schooltie. And dawdled at unbuttoning his shirt. He were a shy lad, and hated getting changed afore others, didn't know where to look, and oh, what if someone *saw* him looking? He were in a right fret already, then, at that sleek Jack Bastable gaily stripping to bare bum, when that... somewhat forgetful scallywag turns to grab his flannel jammie bottoms for stepping into, giving a flagrant display of...

 – *Stamp*, coughs Kit Bastable.

 And rolls his peepers.

• 10

Poor Peter didn't hardly have time though to make sense of glimpsing that black hatchwork of squigglydoodly soulscript on the chest of a scallywag who were of course, in fact, none other than our very own sparkthumbed hellion Flashjack Scarlequin, scamps! No, he'd toot sweet one scamp in a fake 'tache – and monocle now, and a dressing gown as might pass for smoking jacket – taking him by the arm with a *Nothing to be alarmed about, old boy.*

And Peter feels just ever so slight a prick in his thigh, and then suddenly very tired... woozy even. But merrily so.

– Morphine, says a scrag called Squirlet Nicely, just a little later in the girl's room, scowling at Janiemalinky Longpins, the Stamp's fresh-Fixed scofflaw courier. At the tyke now out cold on the rug. At the suitcase Janey slid out from beneath the bed so's Squirlet could find a proper hidey for their precious charge. The Stamp beside it, cause Janie only gone and dropped the case, didn't she, with an almighty thump. So when they flicks on a light to see what's what, there's Lily stood blinking, all, *Whatever is that?*

Cause, yeah, it's Foxtrot and Squirlet, scamps! Duh!

Cause though Foxtrot Wainscot Hottentot III were the savviest scamp ever Fixed, and though Squirlet Nicely had such Mad Skillz at hiding things she run the Opium Trade for centuries, it weren't till they put their heads together, it sparked as how the Land of Somewhere Safe might *not* be so unreachable as a dreamland of legend oughta. Put two and two together they had, and circled on a map, before all em crib bosses, the queerest mix up of highlands and islands and skylands. An island called Skye? That's like a mountain called Ocean, a sea called Desert. Bonkers!

It were a doolally eedjitry, them other bosses says, that just cause they'd banged to rights this *pair of ducks* – as yer calls such muddled-up illogicality – that just cause an island called Skye were *absurd*, they should fancy it a gateway to yer topsy-turvy Cuckooine of whimsy aplenty. But Foxtrot, he'd done his homework, scamps, and why, ain't there a groanhuff tale? Not a *fabble*, true, but with yer Nazis blitzing London, with invasion coming... a shot worth taking, for the safety of the Stamp.

A tale of a Faerie Bridge, no less, a bridge to Somewhere Safe.

Part Two

• 1

It were a misty ochenin on the island of Skye, scamps – yer ochenin being to the dawn as yer gloaming is to dusk, that half-lit time when the sun ain't in the sky no more or yet, but it ain't proper dark yet or no more. A misty ochenin on the 19th of December, only two days to the Winter Solstice, as a boxy black and red van of the Royal Mail rattled along a road a little north of Portree, and parked at a lane for the postie to pop out, pop a letter through the manse's door.

Inside, the Reverend Earnest Blackstone, in his study, heard his letterbox clatter and looked up from the manuscript he'd just set down to work on. A pious Christian allegory his story were, of a magic land where's God were an eagle, where's yer could only enter if yer soul was white, yer blood pure of all corruption. Except Evil had infiltrated, innit, through that slattern Eve's temptation; why, the Father's Land were *overrun* by swarthy hook-nosed goblins and whatnot, so his heroes had to take the throne.

It'd go down a storm with his Christian Cadets, he was sure.

He looked up, and stood up, and merrily whistled a jaunty air from his rambler youth as he strolled his way to the front door to collect this letter – what sparked a peer at some specific nuances to the crossings of the t's in his name, a *recognition*, such that back at his study desk, with the missive

17

unenveloped, unfolded and flattened on his blotter, why, from a drawer now, he brings out the strangest stone, like a flattened doughnut. And he peers through the hole of this Druid's Glass, as they calls it here, to read the *true* message.

And he stands up again, scamps, does Herr *Ernst von Schwarzenstein*. Cause just as that letter had a true message yer might only see by a peep through a Druid's Glass, if yer was to peek back at *him* from t'other side, yer'd see he'd a true *name*, secret agent of the Abwehr that he were, and not just a German spy but one of Himmler's Ahnenerbe, on a mission not just covert but *occult*. And on a new mission now, scamps. Cause in the magical invisible ink he'd read were the message... that the Stamp had come to Skye.

• 2

Where *exactly* that Stamp might be's another matter though, innit. Cause as Lily wakes blearily a bit later, ain't no more sign of that odd stony cylinder than of Squirlet and Janie. Mark my words, it's stashed away somewhere's sneaky as fuck, scamps. But she's such a confuddled memory of last night, Lily's sure she must've dreamt that anyways, so she just slips from bed and swooshes curtains open to gaze out over the Bentley parked below... on a bridge's battlemented pier, scamps, the driveway reaching over a dried-up grassy moat, and out through woods, toward a glorious dawn.

— Red sky in the morning, shepherd's warning, singsongs the plump cook what's dishing out Peter's breakfast kippers, in the kitchen Lily finds her way to by the scrumptious aroma. It seems them Bastables has gone off exploring, eh, and the cook woeful of the consequences, for all's it shows *them* no lazyboneses. Peter rubs his eyes.
— Aren't those Bastables a jolly queer bunch though, says he.
— I should say so, agrees Lily. I'd the queerest dream that quiet one had a *bollard* in her suitcase.
— I'd a funny dream too... But they've the right idea in *exploring*, what?
— I'll say!

Soon as breakie's scarfed then, well, it's off for a nosey round the castle for Peter and Lily too. Down corridors and upstairs and into rooms, they goes, gawping at all the oil paintings, chandeliers and such. And there's oubliettes and towers and everything. But the temptation as makes Lily's nose twitch proper is when she spots in the drawing room... why, it's Lady Fay's snuff tin. And, see, Lily fancies it fun to try a little.

– But you oughtn't steal! says Peter.

– If we're going to have our pockets picked, says Lily, I jolly well don't see why not!

Well now, scamps, there's things yer sniffs as makes yer fly *metaphorickly* speaking. There's black inkies and Tippex, nail varnish and poppers, speed and coke – all sorts! But see, wishsnuff does it *literal* like. And what Lily didn't know as she opened that tin to pinch just a peck of it – just to play, like, in a make-believe as she was the dauntless doyen Her Nibs herself... what she didn't know was that this were no ordinary snuff, not by half. So it were quite a surprise when she sneezes – *atchoo!* – and finds herself three feet off the ground.

• 3

– Do you think Lady Fay's... a *witch?* says Peter as them two skims the hills east of Dunstravaigin, having took off from the battlements an hour ago, bundled up in greatcoats, scarfs and mittens, having rocketed to a nearby white-capped knoll, swooped to scoop handfuls of powdery crunch, having had a ripping aerial snowball fight, relaxing now.

– Beats me, says Lily. I – look!

Down below, where three roads join, ooh, it's the Bastables.

– Quick! Higher or they'll see us! says Peter.

And up they goes, so high even as Janie does look up, all she sees is... whassat?... hawks?

– Oughtn't we go back? says Lily. It's getting awful grey.

And that it is, scamps; yer sky above's right dark now, but Peter's so enjoying it, oh, to fly like a bird, and they've almost crossed the island, and why, look, there's some soldiers out for an exercise – Polish by the uniforms, Lily reckons, except *those* who're Home Guard. Getting a right roasting from their captain too, they are, the two she points out.

– I do wish we could hear what they were say-*aaaaaah-atchoo!*

And by fuck, scamps, suddenly he can, every bleeding word, clear as a bell.

To be sure, he don't aktcherly get much benefit in hearing that bespectacled private and his portly mate apologising to their captain, partly cause one downside of wishsnuff granting such gifts is the depletionary effect on flight, making for a right distracting brown trouser moment as Peter drops fifty feet, and partly cause he's come in at the end of Sir Godfrey's bollocking

19

Goggles and Tubbs for repeating rumours – *rumours* – that the old WW1 internment camp on Raasay is now in use for nabbed Nazi spies.

No, he misses the fortuitous expositional happenstance what might well be relevant laters, scamps.

But it don't really matter anyways, not to Peter, if all he catches is a snatch of summat about Germans on some other island, not half an hour later, when the snowstorm as was threatening before is now full blizzarding and them utterly and hopelessly lost in it, battered by the winds.

– Hold hands, Lily cries, or we shall lose even each other!

But Peter he has a bright idea.

– I do wish I knew where we were, says he.

And with an almighty *AAAAAAAAATCHOO!* he plummets like a stone, Lily dragged down with him, *SPLOSH!* into an icy loch.

• 4

It's a pair of chittery-gnashered shivering tykes, sodden as the snuff in a tin not *quite* airtight, who enters, with a tinkle of bell, a bitter windblast, and a billow of snow around em, the couthy wee tea room in Portree, to no small hullaballoo from three old biddies in a corner and the buxom lassie serving. There's many an *ochone!* and babbling in the Gaelic, even some in English, but them tykes can't be understood *at all* through their clattery stammers. So they's just huchled through to the kitchen stove, half-stripped and blanketed and plonked to thaw.

In a bit, they's warmed enough to whisper panicky between em, cause the lassie's been telephoning round to find who these waifs belongs to, and however shall they explain to Lady Fay? And they don't want to *lie*, Miss Eilidh here's been so nice to em, but they's just dreaming of Dunstravaigin, hot Ovaltine – and *lunch*.

Oh, half the counter through front is a glass case full of jam tarts and tablet and tiffin and turkish delight... but they haven't any money.

– Perhaps if we ask very nicely, whispers Lily.

– I couldn't, says Peter. I couldn't ever be a *scrounger*.

Just then, scamps, there's a tinkle of bell, an icy howl, and who should enter but the Bastables – the scruffs! – the two youngest in front, the elders toddling behind.

– Well, that was a washout, Squirlet's saying.

– Hmmm, nods Foxtrot.

– Faerie Bridge, my arse, says Flashjack. It were a bleeding junction in the middle of fucking nowhere.

– Squirlet, you're sure...? says Foxtrot.

– If you know where to hide things, says she, you know where they're hidden.

– Still, says Flashjack. At least we ain't likely to get invaded by Nazis up here.

– *Don't jinx it, Flashjack,* says Squirlet and Foxtrot whirling together.

Sat through back, amid togs asteam on a clotheshorse by the big iron range, snuff tin sneakily atop it, peeping through the kitchen door and cake cabinet, Peter and Lily ain't too conspickyerous, but still they ducks down, not sure *why* but showing good waif instincts when shit gets weird, eh, to keep yer head down till yer knows what's what. They did both have... *weird dreams* of em Bastables last night, mind. It's weirder still when the icklest Bastable walks right up to Miss Eilidh to order *four teas, please,* in fluent Gaelic. Even Squirlet's taken aback by that.

• **5**

But Foxtrot himself's finding *his* curiosity... quite piqued, for with his interductions of the Bastable clan to Miss Eilidh, and his explifications of their evacuation, it soon comes out there's two bedraggled wretches in back as must be Lady Fay's *other* two charges. And Foxy can't figger how's they got here without passing his team on the road. So he's angling his frown at the kitchen door – was that a sneeze he heard? – but if anyone's back there, they's hid as sneaky as if Squirlet done it.

He don't like it, this new variable to be factored into Operation Faraway.

If he'd harked more'n just peeked, scamps – and let that be a lesson to yer – if he'd targeted his lugs as keen as his peepers, he might have picked up not just one smothered sneeze but two, and some hurried whisperings afore em – *I so wish we were invisible!* and, *I do wish our clothes were dry already!* And he might have heard an excited gasp afters, a hushing, rustlings, and maybe's soon a creak of floorboards, tippytoe footsteps going squeak by squeak by squeak toward the door.

The mousiest whisper, cupped lips to an ear: *the bell.*

But no.

That bell thwarting Lily and Peter's scarpering rings anyways just then though, a dozen twerps piling in boisterous, rifles over shoulders, side caps

on noggins – a squad of Christian Cadets. As clocks our scruffs. And decides they's *collecting money for the Poor Box, cough up*.
– Bad idea, growls Squirlet.
– Impoverished orphan, mate, breezes Flashjack. Ain't got a tosser to me kick.
One twerp makes some jibe at that, as none but Foxtrot would've got the *gist* of even, if that twerp hadn't dropped a *gyppo* into the Gaelic of his snark.
– Ow! says he, sniggers cutting dead. Who kicked me?

As it happens, it were aktcherly Lily done it, cause she'd had such prejudice sneered at her plenty, thanks, yer pigskin twerps then as now suffering fuckincluectomies when it comes to actual *discernment* versus *discrimination*. But even if them scruffs had knowed who dropped em in it, sure as a scofflaw getting stroppy if yer bounces on their bed, they'd have slapped Lily on the back with a *Good show!* and *Nice one!* sure as fuck wouldn't have huffed that it wasn't *them* started it.
No, they was peachy with it being started for em. And happy to finish it.

• 6

They almost *does* finish it, and in five seconds flat, cause the *flash* in *Flashjack* ain't just about his thumbfire trick. He's got a quarter of them twerps decked with a whirl-*whap!*-twirl-*thunk!*-birl-*bonk!* while Foxtrot, Squirlet and Janie's only on their first. Ain't hard to see why yer Stamp's scofflaw courier always has an hellion escort, and why Foxtrot picked Flashjack as hellion *ace* for this mission. Another five seconds and they *would've* finished it, no doubt, but then a voice thunders out to scrunch yer bollocks, even them as hasn't any.
– STOP! THIS! AT! ONCE!

And blow me if them scruffs don't stop dead with fists inches from fizzogs and knees a tick from knackers, even yer most unbossable Scruffian bosses. Bold black against the blizzard, blasting icier than the wind, that Lady Fay don't half know how to make an entrance, and if Peter and Lily had knowed our scruffs proper, they'd have sworn her a witch now for sure.
– Boys, boys, boys, comes a voice behind her though – why, it's the Reverend Blackstone arriving too, word having reached him of two strange waifs in Miss Eilidh's tea room – this is hardly Christmas spirit!

Now them two marches in, with great tuttings – and noticeably frosty glances at each other – and at a quick signal from Foxtrot to play meek, pax is made, hands shook, bloody noses stuffed and, *oh, that should prooooobably get looked at.* And it seems Lady Fay has her Bentley nearby, so it's back to Dunstravaigin, where the Brawling Bastables might redeem themselves by helping her find her snuff tin which – and she says this most hinty indycatively – she must have *misplaced.* Which them scruffs'd find right sporting, as they's bustled off, if they'd a scooby what she was on about.

– Oh, dear, whispers Peter outside. We've landed them right in the drink.
  – They shan't find it, frets Lily. Unless we fly back and hide it pronto!
  But as Blackstone dispatches his twerps homeward to lick their wounds, as our two hovers over his head, they's not the only ones watching them scruffs pile into Lady Fay's car and scheming. For the Reverend rummages from his pocket an odd O-shaped stone that he peers through.
  – Scruffians, he hisses. I knew it! Oh, I'll have their Stamp, and then I'll scrub those filthy scruffs. Or my name isn't *Ernst von Schwarzenstein.*

• 7

– He *must* be a German spy! says Lily.
  – And I doubt it's a bath he means when he says *scrub,* says Peter.
  Weaving the winds of the road, they glides behind Blackstone's car, hand-in-hand so's not to lose each other, that blizzard abated but them still being invisible. Peter feels awful for the fate of them Bastables, surely in the frame for *their* mischief. But this so-called Reverend's clearly got dark designs to put bed-with-no-supper in the pale, so clearing the innocent must wait. Right now there's the nefarious to be rumbled. Foiled even.

– I'll bet that stamp's some Penny Black with a secret message on it, says Lily. I shouldn't be at all surprised if that Kit Bastable collects stamps – oh, and I bet their father sent it to him just before being captured, to keep it safe.
  They floats slowly forward, making sure to linger far enough behind the Reverend, as he tramps through the snow, that it won't be *them* getting rumbled. Out into the wilds he's trekking.
  – And he'll have a radio out here or something, she says, to report back to the Fuhrer. I'll bet you jam on Sundays!

But it ain't no radio that ersatz reverend Ernst von Schwarzenstein is traipsing to, through the blanket of snow left by the storm. No, scamps, but rather, up on that island called Skye, up near Garrafad, there's a little Loch of Enchantment, Loch Shianta they calls it, what's said to heal yer if yer drinks from it and circles three times widdershins, but woe betides any as tries to fish in it. And it's this yer occultist Nazi spy has as his destination, a right fishy customer with fishy business on his mind.

— Whatever is he up to? says Lily.

For it's widdershins he's circling, but walking backwards, incantating all the while's he does it, that there Druid's Glass held to one eye like our Foxtrot's monocle. And don't you imagine him incantating in Latin, scamps, like some Harry Potter *Masturbatorius!* bollocks or all that sadwanky Satanistic tosh going back to some misogynist cuntfucker in yer Middle Ages as had it in for midwives. No, it's an older tongue he's talking, summat Peter ain't been schooled in. Tain't the Gaelic neither, but an uglier guttural cant, rising to a bellow.

And in the loch's dark waters, summat rising with it.

• 8

— I think we'd best scram, says Peter.

— Oh, don't be such a wibbler, Peter, says Lily. We shan't have another chance if we leave now.

— We mightn't have any chance if we stay. I think he's summoning a *monster.*

And he ain't wrong, scamps, cause the magic in that loch come from a creature old as the tongue commanding it, and as Blackstone bellowed, the water rippled and bubbled and churned and roiled, and up from the depths it come, thrashing wild, sloughing and sloshing water from every surface, trickling and dribbling with it, till there it loomed. Indescribable.

Invisible.

Oh, they'd had a *glimpse* of the horror as was the Addanc – cause that's what it were, an Addanc, though whether it were just *an* Addanc, whether it were one thing or many, neither Peter nor Lily could even begin to say. For all they'd seen, scamps, in that glimpse, were the mass of writhings and slother, flurryings and snicketings shaped by the water running off a thing no more visible than they was. Only one there as could see it proper were Blackstone, peering through his Druid's Glass as he paces round it, roaring.

— Addanc! Obey me! Bring me –

But he halts, scamps. And Peter's and Lily's blood runs cold, cause in his circling of the loch, he's on the far side of it now from them, and with his gaze being pointed at the Addanc, it's pointed through and between its weaving squirmeries. And he's raising a finger now – fuck! – pointed straight at them sleuths.

– Seize them! shouts Blackstone.

– He sees us! cries Peter.

But, *no* – Lily *sneezes*. And Peter he sees her! She's visible, nabbable, golly gosh grabbable!

– LILY! he shouts as she *whomps* in the snow.

– Just go, she says. Go, Peter!

Oh, scamps... Oh no.

He flees, does Peter, rockets away in panic. He goes and leaves her.

Fucking chickenshit, eh?

But no, scamps. It ain't as simple as some'd have it. It's a *twerp* who hates boys being *girly*, and from that reckons Peter a cowardy custard. It's a *twerp* who hates girls being *boyish*, and so reckons Lily an uppity bitch who should've scrammed on Peter's word. Fuck that.

If yer don't like it, leg it – first rule of Scruffian Club. But *mind yer mate's back*, that's first rule too, innit?

So when yer in a pinch, yer just takes the plunge, scamps.

• 9

So when Lily wakes with a shriek from a nightmare of cold, wet horrors latching limbs and clamping gob and smothering, engulfing – when she wakes thrashing and flapping to get it off, *get it off*, as she clicks that there ain't nuffink to *get* off, and calms down enough to see she's inside now, in a study, no less, first thing she thinks is to kick herself for getting scrobbled – and what of Peter? Oh, what if he scrobbled Peter too, and all because she wouldn't scram? And fuck it whether she's *right* or *wrong*. Try blaming the fucking scrobbler.

Cause there he's sat, gluggling port from a decanter, smug in an armchair facing the one he's plonked Lily in, a wee table betwixt em, and a desk at the window stacked and strewn with paper, bookcases all around.

– Back with us? says he. You had quite a turn, dear child. What magics *have* you been meddling in? One must be wary of the dark arts, child. Why, had I let you interrupt my exorcism, we might have had a catastrophe.

And oh, the gaslighting that cuntfucker starts on then, playing pious soldier in a war on ancient pagan evils.

He don't know she's got him down for Adolf's arselicker, see. Thinks he can spin her a big fat porkie and fuddle her ickle noggin to help him in his mission. Such heathenry here, says he, like the Faerie Flag of the Clan MacGuffin, a lover's gift from *Titania*, he sneers, waved to summon *faerie* armies, waved twice already, to be taken back the third time with the bearer to *Faerie*. A Banshee's Blessing? A Devil's Bargain, more like! Those *faeries?* Hellspawn!

Weaves in truth, he does, as the sneakiest porkies do, of his *original* mission: to snaffle that flag.

– But these *Bastables*, says he, the ones you... pinched a little magic soor ploom from, perhaps? Or half-inched a pinch of Satan's sherbert, perchance? Far worse. You mustn't trust them, dear child. Look to their chest, you'll see their compact with Old Nick wrought there in black.

Strolled by the desk now in an idle sortie – every inch of instinct in her Scruffian, by fuck – Lily looks up innocently from a map of Skye with *THE BRIDGE?* written beside an X in red ink, at some place called Dun Scaith.

– They're terribly... *queer*, she says.

– *Queer*, sniffs he. Precisely.

• 10

And what's that mousey Peter up to, I hears yer ask, while's Lily's braving the lion's den? While's she's working her mark – even taking stovies and hot cocoa what he rings a bell for his woman to whip up, cause though she don't trust him, not one bit, she can't let him *know* that – where's that cowardy custard scarpered to? Why, he's right outside the window, innit, having got himself safe and turned right round. He's out there right now, cursing himself for a ninny and a sissy, and sworn that, by crikey, he'll spring her first chance he gets.

He's wishing she *were* sprung, natch. He ain't no halfwit, savvies wishsnuff *should* solve this sneezey-peasy. But it ain't bleeding working. Maybe's it's yer Law of Diminishing Returns with elevating sniffables, but maybe's it's more, cause when the bowl drops from Lily's hand, her head plops sleepytime, and his *frantic* wishes does fuck all, well, first tick Blackstone's out the room, Peter's sliding the window up, launching in... finding himself faceplanted on the floor and all too visible.

– Ah, the other, says Blackstone at the door. As I was saying –

– I jolly well don't care! snaps Peter. *Nazi spy!*

So, okay, maybe Peter's not making the *best* snap decisions presently, blowing Lily's charade of incogniscience to fuck here. But it's him who suffers for it as Blackstone snarls:

   – Addanc, take him.

And from nowhere Peter feels it, slithering up his legs, under shorts, under shirt, up his shivering back and clinging there, cold and wet. He reaches round to shove his hands down his collar, scrabbling to claw it off, but his nails just digs into his skin, scratches himself.

   – Now, dear child, you will do what I command.

   – I shan't, cries Peter.

   – You will. Bring me the Stamp.

   – To Dunstravaigin, dear child, croons the unctuous cuntfucker. To your master's bidding.

Then Peter feels the Addanc as skitterings along his sleeves and out the cuffs, as slitherings down his legs, as snakelets around em. Feels it puppet his arms to latch round Lily. He's sobbing, helpless, a dolly in its clutches. And he's out the window, in the air, lurching through it, hurtling, like this *thing* splotched on his back has splattericated out some great mass of monstrous limbs, to hoik itself up, a giant squiddish spidery fuckin nightmare critter, and skitteryslither off into the gloaming.

   Off to Dunstravaigin.

Part Three

• 1

When Lily wakes from her second conking-out in one day – *three* if yer counts Squirlet spiking her – it's to a blur and babble of, *Oh my, laddie! Och, the poor lass! Och, whateffer will Herself say?* then, *To the bath with her! A warm bath and a posset! And let's get some soup in you, laddie!* and she's bouncing away, then wibbly on her pins to get her togs off, then the luxury of it, scamps, the floaty, dreamy, splendiferous luxury of a piping hot bath and spicy hot milk (with rum!) to unbefuddle her till she's herself again.

So presently then, she's snug in nightie, dressing gown and slippers, peeping into the kitchen to find Peter scoffing down his third bowl of cullen skink, and a clean bowl waiting for herself, and Mrs Macleod with a ladle: *In and sit ye down, lass.*

As she tucks in, between slurpy gobblings to make Flashjack look refined, she whispers to Peter.

– However did we get back? How did you get me away from...?

Peter *slooroops* a spoonful of soup and dawdles ever so long over it, before finally gulping.

– The wishsnuff, of course. How else?

He coughs into his hand.

– But whatever did you tell Lady Fay?

– I told her we got a lift halfway to Portree on a tinker's cart, but got caught in the snowstorm after, and ever so lost on the way back – oh, if only we'd just *waited* in that nice tea room. You ought to have heard me, Lily. I should lie for England in the Olympics!

– Oh, you're such a fibber, Peter, but didn't she find the magic snuff? Oh, do tell me she hasn't punished the Bastables.

– She *has*, he laments, and it's still in my pocket. I feel such a rotter.

As the cook pours em a hot toddy each before bed then – what them poor Bastables is already sent to – Lily fills Peter in on all Blackstone's queer talk, and they debates in fierce whispers what's they should do. Should they come clean about the snuff, and spill the beans on Blackstone's schemes? Oh, but can they trust the witch? Can they trust the Bastables? What if it's villains on all sides? *Demons?*

– Marked on the chest? says Peter. So it *wasn't* a dream.

– And I didn't dream that bollard thing either. Peter. That must be this Stamp he's after.

• 2

Ain't nothing decided then and there, cause both them tykes' noggins is awhirl with possibiities. If it were just some Nazi spy after a list of British agents in a microdot on a Penny Black, they mightn't have proof, but they should surely trust the authorities. But when their guardian and fellow charges might be in league with the Devil... The only thing for it's to do some further investigatering, innit. Leastways, that's the consensus they comes to in furtive conspirings in the hall before each slipping into their bedroom.

Lasts all of one sleepless hour for Lily, it does.

– Oh, I can't keep quiet, says Lily after an endless hour of tossing and turning. I can't and I shan't! I won't believe there's even an ounce of truth in that Nazi's rot.

And she sits bolt upright in bed, jumps out, and marches to flick the light switch on, to find Squirlet sat up and peering at her, one hand slipped casually under her pillow – and I'll leave *you* to decide whether it's a syringe or a shiv it's resting on, scamps, or maybe's resting between the two, ready to use either if need be.

– Spill, says Squirlet eventually.

So out it all comes then, how Peter and Lily *knows* there's more to these Bastables, that they're something called Scruffians, aren't they, with strange

29

marks on their chests, and this magical Stamp thing, and – no, they haven't told anyone, why do you ask? – but anyway, there's – is that a screwdriver? – a *Nazi agent* after them to steal it – yes, a Nazi agent! – and he's a monster at his beck and call, and Lady Fay is a witch, they think, with magic snuff that lets you fly and grants you wishes, and *whatever in the goshdarn blazes is going on?*

Five minutes later, she's peeping out the door of the girl's bedroom at Squirlet rapataptapping on the door of the boys'. At Squirlet muttering under her breath as she does it again: rapataptap; rapataptap; rapataptap. Sorta like... *Scruffians STAMP.*

Eventually, the door opens and there's a whingy mumbling from inside: *mmfmmfuck is it?*

– War meeting, says Squirlet. Bring the twerp.

– Stray. Foxy figgers he's a stray.

– Just bring him. Five minutes.

– Are you having a pow wow? says Lily as Squirlet swooshes past.

Squirlet shakes her head, but it's less of a *no* so much as a *for fuck's sake.*

• 3

In the girls' room, in a blanket fort lit by flames from Flashjack's fingertips, them tykes' jaws dropped in cross-pinned laps, Foxtrot savvies Peter and Lily of Scruffians. As he unbuttons his pyjama top to show em his soulscript, he savvies em how once far ago the groanhuffs made a magic doodad called the Stamp, what Fixes yer to stay the same forever, imperishable, ever springing back how yer was Fixed. He slices a shiv across his palm at that, lets em watch the wound heal before their very eyes. Slave labour, they was. Until they nicked that Stamp.

No groanhuffs mustn't *never* get their grubby mitts on that Stamp never again, them two learns, least of all Nazis.

– Like yer bleeding Traitor Prince, says Flashjack. Fuckin sixfingers purple-pissy Saxe-Coburg knobs!

– Infiltration to the highest echelons, alas, says Foxtrot, is what my... somewhat *ardent* confederate here's driving at.

Them tykes don't want to believe it, not in Dear Old Blighty, but their protests gets less huffy as the Scruffians fabbles their histories, gets uneasy at tales of Roma and Jews being preyed upon, gets muted in gobsmack and flabbergast... gets turned.

– Why that's ghastly, sniffles Lily. Ghastly.

***

Peter looks even angstier than her, tortured even, like's he might burst into tears, or burst *out* with summat. But...

– So, he says meek as a mouse, almost biting his words back... wherever did you hide this Stamp?

– Need to know, says Squirlet curtly.

Peter looks away sharpish, beaming red.

– MacGuffin then... ponders Foxtrot after a silence. A wild card...

– No love lost between her and Blackstone, says Squirlet.

– If she hates a Nazi, she can't be all bad, says Flashjack.

– Who doesn't hate Nazis? says Squirlet.

– Ooh! says Flashjack. I know this one! Collaborators!

Squirlet shakes her head. Sighs.

And Foxtrot strokes his 'tache for a while then, Flashjack dances the flames on his fingers, and Peter bites his bottom lip, until suddenly Lily pops from broody hunch to upright.

– Oh, she says. Oh! You were looking for a Faerie Bridge, weren't you? To sneak the Stamp to safety?

Cause in all her babble of Blackstone's schemes, she'd forgot to tell em of the *map* she saw, what had a bridge marked as maybe's at Dun Scaith, on the island's poky-down bit... and Blackstone *was* here about this *Faerie* Flag thing originally.

– A Faerie *Flag*, indeed? says Foxtrot.

• 4

The next morning, what's the day before Midwinter now, after all that conflabbing deep into the night, it's well past dawn by the time Lily toddles down yawning to the kitchen to find Foxtrot and Squirlet up and prattling of their plans for the day – since Lady Fay's gone off already, to help organise the Solstice Ceilidh. And well, they mustn't have a repeat of yesterday's exploratory fiascoes, so perhaps it's best to stay in the castle today. Perhaps they can all play Hide-and-Seek? The Brawling Bastables and the... Oddsorts Other Two together, eh? Once the slugabeds rise?

Cause yeah, as Peter and Janie and (eventually) Flashjack surfaces, and scarfs some scran, and they all adjourns to that nice drawing room for a bit of hush-hush and on-the-QT, it seems now even leery Squirlet's ready to concede that Lily and Peter's hearts is in the right place, and homeless orphans as they are, well, yes, maybe's even Peter's not a twerp after all. As the scouring of Dunstravaigin Castle for that flag gets plotted, why, they's even made honorary cohorts enough for's Janie to tap em on the shoulder, plop their purses in their hands.

– You pilferers! huffs Peter. Rotten pinchers! This is a rum do if ever!
Hands on hips, he stomps his foot, whipples his shoulder from the hand clapped on it, pouty at Flashjack's scallywag unruffle.
– Easy-oasy, mate. She's fresh-Fixed, needed the practise, eh?
– Well, if *you* should have something stolen, Peter grumps, you should jolly well deserve it.
Mind you, his fizzog do flick a bit sheepish soon's he says that.
– Scruffs ain't got fuck all but each other, shrugs Flashjack.
– And *the Stamp*, Jack, says Squirlet.
– Oh don't be so uptight, Peter, says Lily. You look quite beastly.

So it's Flashjack counting to an hundred – which should take a good while with all the restarts, Foxtrot reckons – and the rest of em's off to nosey, with a plan to meet back here on the hour. And Lily looks *very* hard at the first room on her list, but all as seems notable is a mounted bull's head with the motto *Hold Fast*, a framed letter from Sir Walter Scott thanking his hostess for her hospitality, and a collection of antique swords in glass cases. Which are terribly grand, especially the claymore, but guns are more Lily's thing really.

• 5

– Winchesters, Smith and Wessons, and Colt .45s, she's saying to Peter in the drawing room when the grandfather clock chimes. When she were *very* young, see, never knowing her mother, and being raised British as mutton pie, she got *her* type of Indian mixed up with that of cowboys. It were so long ago, she hardly 'members it now, but it made her so want to ride horses and shoot guns, and why couldn't *Tonto* be The Lone Ranger? she'd wondered at that movie serial where's the villain's trying to figger which of five Texas Rangers is the masked hero.

– Anything? Foxtrot says as he paces into the room, interrupting her blether. With his monocle in his eye now for extra peeper power, and his hands clasped behind his back under the paisley dressing gown he's popped on over his togs, he's looking right Sherlock Holmesy.
Peter and Lily shakes their heads – no luck. Janie holds out her cupped

palms with a dead mouse in em.
– Yes... well, says Foxtrot.
– Eighty-eleven, says Flashjack, eighty-twelve...
– You *can* stop counting now, old chap, says Foxy.
– Oh, thank fuck, says Flashjack.
– Well, I suppose we'll just have to hope... ah, Squirlet.

And here's Squirlet now, who's had more of a score. A proper *method* has Squirlet, see, working in reverse from the last place anyone would look to the first. First place *she's* looked is the place *she'd* hide it, which is the *best* possible hidey, natch – well, after wherever she's stashed the Stamp. If yer knowed that Dunstravaigin Castle like the back of yer hand, yer'd still never guess it, and she won't tell em where, so's not to give away her secrets, but she's had a wee shufty there, and did find *summat*, albeit not what they's looking for.

It's a silver chanter, scamps, as yer might poke in yer bagpipes or play as hornpipe. *The* Silver Chanter, story goes, of a MacGuffin who was so mopey over doing everyfink rubbish, the Faerie Queen took pity, give him a choice of blessings: to sail any ship; to win any battle; or to play the pipes. Chose the pipes, he did, and quite right too.
– Ooh, can I see? says Peter. I love the recorder.
And he gives it a little tootling what makes Flashjack jig. Literally. As in, *Me legs have gone barmy!*
– Hold on to that, says Foxtrot.

• 6

Well, it's clear now that while's *Peter* do seem to have put his heart into the search, (though he don't seem terribly proud when's Foxtrot commends him for it,) the others is so distractable and unproductive, Squirlet's only gonna has to do their bleeding snooping all over again, innit, to make sure them amateurs hasn't missed owt. Even Foxtrot spent his whole hour eliminating every single book in one library bookcase as lever for a secret passage. So, she's all, *Just... follow me and stay out of my way*, and they's off in a new game of Follow-My-Leader.

Through all the maze of Dunstravaigin Castle they skips in single file behind her, Flashjack cheerily continuing the song as he keeps edgy at the door of each room while's the rest loiters like lummoxes, agawp at Squirlet's meticulosity and imaginativity. Takes *ages*, but eventually they's down to what's she deems the *amateur hour hideys*, and blimey if her tappetytapping at the back of a wardrobe cleared of a thicket of fur coats don't betray a false back Squirlet jimmies open to reveal... another fur coat.

– Ooh, can I see? says Lily, for its wintery silver is terribly frontiersman trapper.

Now the Silver Cloak of the Otter King ain't no mundane mantle, as yer might guess from that grand nomenclature, scamps. So, just as Peter piping the Silver Chanter had an unforeseen effect in making Flashjack jig, so too did Lily donning that coat make for quite the gobsmacker. Cause no sooner's it on than it's wrappling round her, squeezing to her body – *Whatever's happening?* – her limbs – *Oh, help!* – her noggin even. It's swallering her up, scamps! Stretching and swaddling, and squooshing her shape now, legs and arms shrinking, body slinkying, whiskers plinking from perkying snoot, till's she's stood there transformogrificated.

– I'm an otter, laments Lily. Oh, no. But I don't want to be an *otter*.
– Yer the cutest thing ever! squees Flashjack. Ooh! Can we see yer crack a shell on yer chest with a stone? Can we? Can we? It's so cute!
– Shut up! says a most miffed Lily. I'm not cute. Am not.
– You really are quite adorable, says Foxtrot.
– *Shut up!*
– Oh, look at your little paws, coos Peter.
– *SHUT UP!*
– Boys! says Squirlet. Then slaps Janie's hand as it reaches down to pet ickle ottery Lily's fuzzy bonce. *Everyone*, she says.
– Quite, quite, ahems Foxtrot. Priorities.

• 7

– Well, I think it's a very poor show, you lot, sulks Lily some time later. I bet it won't *just wear off*, it's not *barely noticeable*, and I shan't *look on the bright side*. If you all think being an otter's *not the end of the world*, you try it.
– We did all give it our best shots, says Peter. There's not even a hint of a seam.
– I'm still not sure you were really looking.
– We *weren't* just tickling your tummy, honest. Cross my heart. We could try the wishsnuff again?
– A flying otter isn't any less an otter.

See, the thing about yer magic, scamps, is it *don't* foller its own rules, and it *don't* always come with a price like yer groanhuffs' fuddy-duddy correctitude make-believes it. If it follered rules and had fallouts for all its impacts, it'd just be bleeding science what we don't know yet, innit! And no, magic is *power*. It's what tromps all over rules, doing what it likes, and it's just a matter of which magic's most bullish as decides in a clash. And a tyke's fancy ain't much cop against some grand nomenclatured MacGuffin *Relic*. So Lily were fucked.

So, all's she and Peter could do was keep poking and prodding and pulling, with much ouching and grouching on her part, while's them scruffs struck on with their mission, the quest for the Faerie Flag what'd led em finally back to that drawing room, to the glass case as was labelled *The Faerie Flag*, yer hiding *in plain sight* being in Squirlet's *too blooming obvious* ranking of sneaky hideys. Which yer might think her daft for delaying till now, but it weren't like the ratty scrap of tattered linen in that case were yer actual Faerie Flag, of course.

No, but with Foxtrot puntied up by Flashjack to pick the lock, with the velvet cushioned backboard that raggedy sham were pinned to gently prised out and took to the grand piano to be laid on its lid, Peter and Lily stopped their fussy footerings to rubberneck, and come scurrying and bounding respectively, Lily scrambling a spiral up Flashjack to his shoulder to see. For there pinned to the back of the backboard were a banner of a cloth as shimmery as silk, in a rainbow of colours what swirled before their very eyes, dazzling.

The Faerie Flag were found.

• 8

By now it's near enough teatime though, scamps, and no sooner have they snaffled their prize than there's the purr of one black 1939 Bentley pulling up outside, and there's a rush to the window alcoves of the drawing room – what's each big enough for a sofa and a couple of armchairs themselves – and a press of noses to glass.

– It's Lady Fay, says Lily, her wee otter whiskers twitching.
– Squirlet, says Foxtrot. Hide the –
But when they turns back to where Squirlet's still stood at the grand piano, that flag's already vanished, and fuck knows where she's planked it.

There's the dummy flag still to go back though, and as Flashjack whaps it in, Janie smacks his bonce and twirls a finger: other way up! They can hear

Herself now, in the door and calling the cook, asking where they's at. As they clicks the glass case closed, she's creaking the stairs, footsteps closing even as Foxy unpicks the lock. Why, it's seconds to spare, then Lady Fay breezes in with an *Hello, hello! No misadventures today, I hope!* to find four Bastables sat on one sofa, Peter miming *Gone with the Wind*, and – Squirlet's hand darts – a cushion.

It's easy enough fabbling Lady Fay that Lily's come down with an awful cold from yesterday, took to her bed, poor thing, but it takes all Foxtrot's skills at flimflam and bamboozling to finagle her from calling a doctor, sending supper up, or popping her head in the door at least – *We'll buck her up, laddie! Fortify her!* Still, with all hands on deck for an impromptu running of his Three Prisoners Monte scam, as requires five wire coathangers, three pillows, two cans, some string, and a turnip, they even manages to scrape through her insistence on a bedtime goodnight.

With a little wait then for things to quiet down, it's time for another War Meeting, all of em gathered in the girls' room again since Squirlet's smuggled up three Ordnance Survey maps from Lady Fay's library so's they can figger out where this Dun Scaith is. Flappled open by Flashjack, spread out on the rug and lined up by Janie, they cover half the floor. Lily scampers round and across the paper.
  – There it is, she says, on the poky-down bit, just like I told you.
  – Sleat, says Foxtrot. And not easy to get to.
But it's there.

• 9

So, with the Stamp under threat from a Nazi agent as has abominable forces under his thrall, there's talk of scarpering right this bleeding second, not least cause Flashjack snorted most of Squirlet's... *pixie dust* keeping edgy all last night and don't fancy another long watch. But even with the wishsnuff, no, reckons Foxtrot, it's too risky at night and as the crow flies. They'll wait for first light, take the safest course: follow the road through Struan and Sligachan, round to Broadford and halfways down to Armadale before cutting across. Fifty miles, he figgers with a bit of string.

  – If we're to set out so very early, says Peter, perhaps we should pack everything we need tonight?
  – Good thinking, dear chap, says Foxtrot. Flashjack, raid the kitchen, rustle us up some sandwiches and a thermos of tea, won't you?

– Jam and Marmite or cheese and marmalade?
– Bit of everything?
– Right-ho. I'll make some coffee for meself as well, shall I?
– Sorry, old chap. I did warn you to pace the coke.
– Where's the fun in that?
– Squirlet, Janie, if you can find a rucksack for the Stamp and the flag...?
– On it, says Squirlet.
– Peter? Come with me.

– I'll stick with my coat and scarf, thanks, says Peter. I can jolly well do without being turned into some beast. Sorry, Lily.

Provisions plonked on a dresser, Flashjack rummages the furs dumped on the floor by Foxtrot and Peter – *Oooh!* – pulls out an ankle-length coat as looks like wolf fur, only reddish. Looks glum when he slings it on and ain't transformogrificated. The black coat Janie fishes out is... fuck knows what, but Squirlet snaffles herself a squirrel fur hat, natch, whiles Foxtrot drapes a foxfur stole on his noggin like a cowl.

– Spiffing, says he.

Lily harrumphs.

So with all in order, they settles down, Flashjack in a chair with the rucksack under it, coffee in hand, Peter and Foxtrot top to toe in Lily's bed, Squirlet and Janie each in their own, and Lily curled up in the rest of the furs, some ottery instinct making that feel rightest. Snug too, it is, so she's almost asleep when's she hears Peter rustling out of bed, whispering to Flashjack how's he's forgot summat.

The sound's so faint when it starts, she nearly don't notice it, the mournful pipe melody, so soft and soothing... the scallywag stretching... yawning...

• 10

What it were as woke her, scamps, we won't never know. It's a mighty power, the magic of the Silver Chanter. If it weren't, why, Flashjack might have a scallywag's skill in sleeping through a bleeding riot once he's out, and a scofflaw will go back to sleep on principle, but yer Foxtrot and Squirlet is a scamp and scrag with centuries of springing out of bed, shivs ready for the waiftakers, at a clink of a link of chain in the streets outside. And they didn't stir. So what sprung Lily from that Silver Chanter's spell is anyone's guess.

It weren't the sudden silence when that tune cut off, not coming to an end

37

gentle as its start, but stopping dead, like as the player just couldn't play no more, just *couldn't*, it had to be enough. Weren't the squeak of the door or the creak of tippytoe footsteps on floorboards as Peter crept back into the room. Weren't the shuffly rustle of clothes as he got dressed, nor of the rucksack being slid from beneath the chair. Weren't the clop of boots knocked together as Peter picked em up. Weren't the squeak of the door as he left.

It weren't the sound of Peter crying through all of this. Weren't the deep breathy sniffs of stifled sobs, the sounds he made when the spasms lurched in him, waves of wailing trying to break loose, and he'd to clamp down to not bawl out aloud, only getting what air he could into his lungs between them wracking shudders. Weren't the soggy snuffles, when wiping his runny nose, like his eyes, with the back of his hand weren't enough, and he'd to snort it clear, quiet as he could. No, Lily slept sound through all that, as they all did.

But wake she did, at *summat*, and saw the scallywag slumped in the chair; and there weren't a nightlight on or nuffink, cause Flashjack had his thumb for candle if need be and the others'd kip better in darkness, but the moon was out and her otter eyes was keen, so she saw that the rucksack weren't beneath the chair no more, and Peter weren't in bed. And she *did* hear summat then, and darted after it, out into the hallway and along it, bounding, downstairs, downstairs, to the front door and a glimpse: Peter hurtling off into the night.

Part Four

• 1

Oh, the moon might have been out that night, and brilliant white in the clearest sky, scamps, and all the stars might have been sparkling bright, the Milky Way itself twinkling so magnificent yer can't hardly imagine, those of yer what's never left London till today. And all that celestial resplenditude might have been shining down upon an island called Skye as was swathed in snow and gleaming back as if in competiton, but as bells tolled midnight all across the land, at the tick as marked it now the Solstice... it were a dark, dark night for Peter Dearest.

Surely he didn't whoosh through the air by wishsnuff, scamps, but hurtle in the Addanc's thrall, eh? Surely it puppeted him to play the pipes and nick the Stamp, then skitteryslithered him away, just a helpless ragdoll in its grip? Oh, if only. If only it'd been just his limbs that dread thing danced, why then that day he might've blurted his burden, blinked his peepers in Morse Code, wept a single tear to warn em scruffs of his plight, done *summat*. But an Addanc on yer back, scamps, oh, that cold wet horror seeps deep, clamps round yer heart.

So it'd slothered his heart in despair and shame, wormed its writhings into him, found a disgust to feed on, to fuel. *Sissy*, it hissed inside him. And the way that bastard Blackstone thought to gaslight Lily, *it* worked its wickedry on Peter, with a warpy lying fuckery that he were too weak to fight, which made the shame worse, which proved he were weak. A vicious cycle it were, scamps, and that were the true dark power of the Addanc, that it could make

39

him do the master's bidding, betray them scruffs, simply because he thunk himself wretched wimpy.

It didn't *need* to puppet him then, hurtle him off the front steps of Dunstravaigin Castle into the sky and away. That were the darkest thing in the dark of that Longest Night for Peter, that he'd just buckled and obeyed, not digging his heels in on the step, not clinging to the doorframe. No, he just opened the wishsnuff tin with hands so trembly he fumbled the first pinch – oh, how useless he was! So he just pinched another peck – how rotten and useless he was! And he give his nose a wipe, sniffed that wishsnuff, and was off.

• 2

North east he flies now, scamps, and he ain't even sure now if it's the Addanc guiding him or some silent wish of knowing where he's going, what he's doing. Out he flies over them hills he skimmed with Lily, but not due east for Portree, no, on a norther course, from the shores of that loch Dunstravaigin Castle looks out over toward the peninsula of Duirinish, northeast across the peninsula of Waternish what Duirinish sprouts out of, across Loch Shizort Beag to Trotternish what Waternish sprouts out of, across the great rising ridge as is the backbone of Trotternish.

It ain't nearly so long a route as that planned by the scruffs to Dun Scaith, but here's a curious thing, scamps, as might make yer wonder if maybe Peter weren't such a basket case as he thunk, cause the first half of his flight takes a good two hours, but from there going halfways of what's left takes another two, and the next halfways takes the same again. To be sure, he's nearly there by the *next* halfways, but by now, why, there's that half-light of ochenin out to the east, over the sea and beyond the mainland.

So maybe's there's hope for him, scamps, even if Peter don't know it yet, in how for all's he knows himself doomed – just *knows* it – he still goes slow to his gallows. Yer might even say he drags his heels when's he's touched down at the coast, near Invertote. He is *hopeless*, eh, so it only makes sense how's he takes *soooo* long on the trail down to the beach, steps so cautious over the treacherous holes between boulders as slickly cold and wet as the Addanc upon him. Even as he comes to the False Church, maybe's there's hope.

He don't *think* there's hope as he comes to the jagged Eaglais Bhreugach, that forty foot high crag bored through by a cave, where's in olden days they roasted cats for the rite of Taghairm. He don't *think* there's hope, seeing Blackstone unbind a blindfold as he rises from a great stone slab at the door, where's he'd lain himself to sleep through the dark of the Longest Night, when the Land of Nod has all the hours, dreaming a glorious vision of his Father's Land. As he holds out the rucksack, Peter just *wishes* there was hope, bitterly. Fiercely.

• **3**

Nine o'clock, scamps. It's an hour since our traitor Peter delivered the Stamp to his master, in treason and treachery, and oh, how it burns in him, his bastardy betrayal. Huddled in the dank cave he sits, hunkered down, hugging his knees, hid from a sun what's only now rising. He should flee as the coward he is, he thinks, dart past Blackstone, scramble over the rocks, away. No, he should shove Blackstone to slip on the wet rock, grab back the wishsnuff snatched with the chanter in a ransack through Peter's pockets, to fly – and take the Stamp too.

Ten o'clock. But what the fuck they waiting for, scamps? In the Addanc's grip, Peter's just wrestling with his misery, but Blackstone...? Oh, he has a plan. Cause his squad of twerps, his Christian Cadets, they's out on an orienteering exercise, innit, one that'll lead em right here... to the Stamp. Only it's not Scruffians he'll be Fixing, Blackstone gloats to Peter, oh no. It's *Uberjugend* he'll be making of em.
Imperishable. Loyal. Crusaders for correctitude.
– They won't follow a Nazi spy! says Peter. They're British!
– Won't they, dear child? says Blackstone.
And he twirls the chanter in his hand.

Eleven o'clock, scamps. Nah, let's calls it oneteen, eh? Oneteen o'clock, and though the sun ain't even at the nowhere-near-overhead as is noon on the Shortest Day, for all's it's at its weakest of the whole year, there's a heat in Peter now, scamps, a *fire*. He's spent a long time raging at himself for what he's done, fucking *fuming*, and now's there's plenty of fire to go round, at the bombs as took his mum and his home, at the fates what brung him here, at Blackstone and his blasted monster.
Yes, he thinks. *Blast* that monster.

Midday.
– Let! Me! Go! shouts Peter.
He thrashes in Blackstone's grip, thrashes against the wild thing, pinned

41

and flailing, between his back and the rock, so wild he can't tell if it's furious to retake him or escape.

– Hold him! roars Blackstone. I command you!

But it's gone, scamps, squirmed loose to squither away, and Peter's shouting *Ha!* in Blackstone's face – till a backhand smacks his gob.

– You *will* play the chanter.

– No, I ruddy well won't, spits Peter.

Another backhand sends him sprawling, and Blackstone towers over him now, murderous, seething.

Simmering down. Growling though gritted teeth:

– No. Matter.

• 4

– Plan A, says Blackstone, smirking.

He turns, steps out to meet the dozen twerps now scrambling over rocks toward the crag.

– Well done, boys, he calls, well done.

Bundled back into the cave's shadows, dumped there on his side, Peter squinches to peek round the reverend's rucksack, mumphing yowly warnings muffled by the gag. He struggles in his ropes like Houdini himself. Only burns his wrists.

Out on that great stone slab, Blackstone unscrews the lid of a thermos flask.

– A sip of hot cocoa to warm you? Might be a wee splash of something in there, eh, wink, wink!

Oh, if only he'd a penknife, thinks Peter, to tease from his shorts pocket with finger and thumb, to saw his bonds. If only he could inchworm across the cave, while Blackstone's busy, to the shelf of rock that ruddy Nazi's sat the chanter and wishsnuff on, heave himself over and get his lips to the pipe, whistle a shrill alarm to rouse them Christian Cadets now sprawled all across the bouldery beach. Or smack the wishsnuff off its perch so's it whacks open on the ground and...

Oh, but it ain't like them movies, scamps. That shit ain't happening.

So he can't do nuffink except scowl and yowl more through the hankie in his gob and rope betwixt his teeth, in language his dear mum would've had his guts for garters for. He can't do nuffink as Blackstone gazes at the setting sun, checks his watch and turns, picks his way over the cave floor's slips and bumps to ferret a torch from his rucksack. Out to the shore goes Blackstone then. And Peter can't do nuffink but watch him point that torch out to the sea and flash it, signalling... a shape in the water.

A U-Boat.

To try the chanter on them Christian Cadets, Blackstone grandiloquises while's he's waiting for them Nazi sailors to row their rubber dinghies ashore, that were but a whim, an *experiment,* as he'll get round to in good time. No, indoctrination back in the Fatherland were always Plan A for these future Uberjugend spies – assuming *this* experiment works. The Stamp must be tested, naturally, before's they uses it on the SS, and the Gestapo, and High Command.

– The Fuhrer first, naturally, he says.

– With only one bollock and that mug-slug over his mush? Be better off Fixed with the shits, mate.

• 5

And it's flipping Flashjack, innit, flipping in with a tumble under a Luger whipped out from Blackstone's coat. Flashjack shooting one hand up to snatch that pistol, shooting one foot out to *BOOF!* Blackstone in his guts, to send him flying. Flashjack rising on one leg, lowering the other, dropping a molten lump of Nazi gun to splat and hiss on wet rock. It's Flashjack to the rescue – and Lily too, nibbling through Peter's ropes so's suddenly he's loose, ripping gag from gob.

– However did you find me? he gasps.

– That little pinch of wishsnuff you left! Oh, quick thinking, Peter!

And they ain't as nimble as an otter or a Flashjack, but here comes Squirlet, Foxtrot, Janie too. Ain't no time for Peter to 'splain how, um, he weren't aktcherly kidnapped though, cause Blackstone's back, swinging a flagpole hunted down by em twerps in their orienteering, brung by em without guessing its part in Blackstone's plans: an axle for the Stamp, for its rolling over their chests to read and write em.

– Ooh! I'm having that, says Flashjack.

And with a scallywag's somersault, handclamp and headbutt, Blackstone's staggering backward, and Flashjack's twirling that flagpole overhead like some fucking Shaolin Majorette.

– ADDANC, roars Blackstone though, fingerpoint targeting. SEIZE THESE –!

– NO! cries Peter, launched at ramming speed, bonce first, *BAM* into

Blackstone's belly.

But too late, scamps. WHACKETY! THWACKETY! SHLOOPETYSPLACKETY! Them scruffs attacking goes flying like skittles, and Flashjack's smacked back, he's sideswiped, whiplashed, flailed in its grasp.

Can an Addanc latch on a scruff's dischuff though, scamps? Can it fuck! Can it worm in to warp yer will with wickedry? Not bleeding likely! Them scruffs is Fixed – resilient, resolute, *resistant*. It can pummel and tangle, all round and invisible, their shivs slashing blindly, but it can't nab and nobble em, ha!

So it's another tack for Blackstone as Flashjack breaks free in a pirouette to strike pose, bo staff flagpole pointed a tick at the Nazi – just for flair, like – then whirling again as he advances.

– ADDANC, bellows Blackstone, and sics it on them senseless twerps now, to wrapple their slumpen flesh, latch into dullwitted dreams, sluggardly hearts. Behind the scruffs on the beach, like zombies they rise, like floppety clockwork toys in a nipper's grip, lolloping at em. While's behind Blackstone on the shoreline, jackboots splash in surf. Mausers point: *Hande hoch!*

Five hands and one paw flicks the vickies.

• 6

Back into that cave of the False Church they dives for cover, scamps, as them Mausers opens fire. Being Fixed, yer might spring back from having yer head blown off, but it ain't fuckin ice cream in the park, is it? And all em holes a machine-gun puts in yer Stamp, the random fuckery of tweaking... well, yer saw how's Quippersnap were after that raid. Fucking half a day of staples and superglue to get his face...

Anyways, there's the Stamp planked in that cave, in the rucksack Janie grabs now – and oh, the chanter and wishsnuff, Peter minds.

– Guard the Stamp! shouts Foxtrot, and Janiemalinky's legs bestrides it, them other longpins of her monicker readied, the fourteen inch steel spike of a rapier-sharp knitting needle in each fist. To the landward exit it is for Foxtrot and Squirlet though, atop the stone slab, side-by-side, first and only line against the Addanc's puppets. To the seaward side it is for Flashjack, lobbing the flagpole back to Peter – *Catch!* – hunkering down to grab a stone, superheat it in a hand white-hot now, fire it. Blackstone ducks, but it makes smashed flaming horror of one stormtrooper's fizzog.

***

From this front to that, Peter looks, at Foxtrot and Squirlet slashing and stabbing, at Flashjack ducking out to fire stone after stone, dancing bullets, pausing to pick a stone, feel its heft, eyeball its shape – why's he ruddy well dawdling? – then he whirls to fire it, but *past* them Nazis now, out to sea, skipping, skimming the waves.

He's only going for the bleeding U-Boat!

But what can Peter do? He looks to Janie, to Lily, back to the Addanc's puppets... and beyond.

Then to the wishsnuff.

Oh, he has a ripping idea, does Peter. Jolly well *ripping*.

Out over them twerp's heads rockets Peter, even as the sub goes boom – *YAY!* – as a bullet in the bonce sends Flashjack birling – *NOES!* Over the Addanc, landing beyond it, amongst the scattered kit: rucksacks and rifles.

Yeah... *rifles*. To his shoulder goes one, aimed for the cave where's two silhouettes struggle. But there's twerps in his path, Foxtrot and Squirlet, and he's no sharpshooter. Oh...

Weaving legs, bounding boulders, darting spry, it's Lily now, dodging magnificent, pouncing to thump his other shoulder, scrambling round his back, clamping and twisty to sight down the barrel: *left a bit! more! NOW!*

• 7

CRACK! As Blackstone spins, Janie makes her break, leaping for the stone slab, rucksack in hand. Frantic and fierce, Foxtrot mutters summat at her. Squirlet turns, locks peepers with him, nods – *our only chance* – and hollers:

– Flashjack! Flagpole!

A shape! Diving through the dark of the cave now, rolling out with the flagpole in one hand, pole-vaulting over them and whirling his staff to rattle bonces like a stick along railings, sweeping the arc of space he lands in. Flashjack tosses the flagpole back over his shoulder for Janie, hunkered over the open rucksack now, to catch.

– Square go.

As Janies lashes the Faerie Flag to that pole then, it's Squirlet and Foxtrot what spins to defend as Blackstone comes roaring at em, winged but rallied. Shivs swish and slice, but he's a trained spy, Blackstone, Nazi fucking James Bond, and he blocks, dodges, swings, blocks. Only another *CRACK!* from the rifle, ricocheted off the crag, breaks his attack, and another *CRACK!* drives him back.

– ADDANC! he booms, in the hollow of the False Church.

From beyond that crag it rises, a dangling of dead Nazis in spear formation, then Blackstone behind, arms raised to heavens.

– Go! shouts Peter.

Them scruffs looks to Peter, to Lily on his shoulder guiding – *Up! To the right!* – at the invisible Addanc puppeting stormtrooper corpses, hoisting Blackstone high like as it's wrappled serpenty round his legs. Back at them not-so-imperishable orphans.

– Come on! they cry.

Lily's off in a jiff, diving to dart through legs, bound rocks again, to the slab. Not Peter though. He scowls at Blackstone.

– I do wish my aim were better, says he.

Atchoo!

And he aims square between Blackstone's eyes, coolly fires. And misses.

Shoulda specified *good*, see. Unfortuitously, *better* here's just leveling up to *shite*.

– Fly, Peter! Fly! cries Lily.

And he's snorting as he runs, rocketing forward as the flagpole rises, oh but low, so even as he's nearly there, a puppeted hand latches on his boot. But Lily's bounding along Flashjack's arm – *The rifle! Reach it out!* – and as he thrusts it forward with just the butt in one hand, Lily's near leaping from Flashjack's hand to snatch the barrel between her ickle paws, her tail only nabbed at the last instant by a scallywag with lightning reflexes, as under the last glint of sunset, Janie waves the flag.

And the world transforms.

• 8

No Faerie Queen comes to help em in their battle, nor to take the Flag back to Faerie with her – like yer groanhuffs' travesty of fabbling's ever right – but instead it's like that flag's headed home itself and taking em with it, into time gone mad. The sun zips a day's arc through the sky, zooms back, across another's path, light slicing a midnight noon where's stars wheel clockwise and widdershins. The moon flickers everywheres, gibbous, crescent, full. Clouds swirl the heavens, closing in to an 'urricane of autumn leaves, bumblebees, snowflakes and cherry blossom. It's a maelstrom of seasons.

See, scamps, it ain't so much the Land of Nod is where yer wishes comes true, simple pimple, cut and dry, more as it's where they comes *alive,* wild and free, yer desires in flesh, showing emselves to yer, all at once. Imagine the whole world were a mirror what yer looked into yer own peepers with, into yer soul itself. It's what yer might see in there the Land of Nod makes real, the part of yer as loves kicking autumn leaves, and the part as loves snowball fights, and how the fuck does it know to choose one?

They're the centre of it all, the Flag, the scruffs, then Lily with rifle as lifeline, Peter clinging on, the hand clamped on his boot, and – he looks back – them puppeted twerps all latched to each other now. Another glimpse of the Addanc's horrors beyond, in the hollows of hail and dandelion seeds and conkers battering it. He's its anchor in the whirlwind. Blast! And past Lily, Flashjack, the scruffs round the Flag, Blackstone clings to the crag.

    – Foooooooxy, says Flashjack, I think we're taking the whole bleedin island with us.

    – Or the island *is* the bridge, muses Foxtrot. Intriguing.

And it's tightening in to swaller em now, that tornado of time, freezing wintery pea-souper one sec, shimmery summer haze the next, rain in Peter's eyes, pollen in his nose – oh, he jolly well better not sneeze. He feels its pull on his feet, not just a hand, but the storm itself, like it's trying to peel him away into some dream of a *particklar* spring day as'll just be *his*.

    – Peter! cries Lily. Your clothes!

His greatcoat's gone, flickered into... silvery onesie?

    – Well, I... never?

The sight of an otter in an ickle cowboy hat is stranger still.

• 9

And now, scamps, now, it ain't just time and togs transforming, cause all of a sudden Peter feels the twerp's grip gone, and he's tumbling forward, heaved into the huddle by Lily and Flashjack, and looking back at a stramash of Christian Cadets all trying to clamber over one another to reach the Flag, and each, one by one, going *whoomf! poof! sploof!* into clouds of midges. Cause that's what a twerp is inside, scamp, all petty spites and hungers at odds with each other and not a jot of integrity to hold em together when push comes to shove.

– Fuck me! cries Squirlet pointing. Look!

    And up on the crag, Blackstone's lion's head roars, his eagle wings beat.

    And Squirlet growls.

    Peter don't know why. Them other scruffs, they savvies it from the fabble of the Stamp's theft, what were in its vault. But Squirlet *was there*, she *saw*, and she minds that monstrous statue, lion-headed Mithras with Moloch to one side, Mammon on t'other. Mithras, born on the 25th of December. Mithras, whose cultists hoodwinked Christendom into birthday parties for him.

Mithras, god of Roman legions and their bundled sticks – them *fascii* – as give fascists their name.

Great eagle wings beat. Forward he pushes. But Blackstone's fighting the whirl of seasons, and even as he manages a step, it's like... some afterimage stays in place. A trail of em he leaves behind with each lurch onward, and as hailstones batters one, rain soaks another, they all pauses, looks around, befuddled. Why, he's only coming unstuck in time! Like as he don't love *any* season, not really, not *actual* nature, just the notion of it, so the Land of Nod it's *trying* to find a time to fit him, but it ain't succeeding.

And Foxtrot...

– Summer! shouts Foxtrot.

– Wish for summer! he shouts.

CRACKOOM! It's like some waltzer blew a fuse, brakes locking, blockaged, buckling, stopped dead, throwing all its cars and all the nippers in em six ways to Sunday. It's like strings held all em scraps of season in that hurricane, and every one of em just snapped. So off them winter days and autumn months goes flying: WHOOOSH! And Blackstone whirling with em too... *awaaaaaaay.*

Then suddenly it's just the six of them, on a glorious summer's day, and of course...

Flashjack slaps at his cheek, wipes summat off his fingers.

– Fuckin midges, says he.

• 10

First thing Peter notices, plonked on his arse on the stone slab, ain't the roasty-toasty warmth of the sun, nor the robin's egg blue of the sky, nor the lushness of vegetation up past the beach's soft white sands, the flowery and fruit-filled foliage as is now veritably *verdant*, headed more for Hesperides than Hebrides. No, it's Lily stood between his legs, her stetson cocked, holding a sharpshooter's rifle, barrel longer than Janiemalinky's legs, and butt customised to fit to an ickle otter's shoulder so's it looks even longer still.

– *Springfield Trapdoor*, she croons in wide-eyed awe.

***

She's not the only one what's had their clobber customised to some inner caprice, scamps. No, them scruffs has too, cause blow me, but ain't Janie looking quite the knight in her shining armour, with Faerie Flag as banner, them two longpins now crossed swords on her back. And Flashjack, he's a dandy highwayman, domino mask and all. Squirlet, she's covered head to toe in the black silks of a ninja, only her eyes peering out, leery as ever. And Foxtrot, why, he's in pirate's pantaloons and billowy shirt, the swankiest swashbuckler, with a rapier Errol Flynn would die for.

That ain't even the end, though, cause all them furs they'd snaffled for their mission, well, maybe's it were the scruff's whims worked em into these guisings, or maybe's a little of the beast was left in em what wanted in on the fun, but now both Squirlet and Janie has tails, they do – squirrel and spider monkey – swishing this way and that. And Foxtrot has fox ears atop his noggin now, flicking that way and this.

– Ooh! What am I? says Flashjack, spinning in search of a tail, tongue lolling down past chin from a gob fierce with canines.

– Mmmmfffmmf mmffmm mm? says Peter.

Leastways, as best the others can tell, that's what he says, voice muffled under the goldfish bowl helmet what goes with his silvery spaceman clobber. At Foxy's miming, Peter savvies what's what – *aaaaah* – and unlatches his helmet, takes it off.

– Whatever are you staring at? says he.

Squirlet taps her forehead, points, and he reaches, feels the pointy ickle horns what's sprouted on his own. From a greatcoat made of wool maybe's. Ickle lamb's horns.

– Well, *I* think you all look *adorable*, says Lily.

Oh, if ever an otter could look smug, scamps. If ever.

Part Five

• 1

With Blackstone and his Addanc strewn to time's winds, so's it seems, leaving just yer odd Nazi bodypart littering the sand, for all's there's hours of playlight left in yer summer afternoon sun, Foxtrot figgers they best stash the Flag back in the rucksack with the Stamp and go noseying sharpish, see if they can't find Keen and Able's crib. Best *ask* hospitality – *good form and all, no?* Land of Nod's open to all slumbering scruffs, sure, but *they* ain't asleep; and every groanhuff's nightmare being one of Keen's hellion guardians, well... best not be *presumptious* of their privileges, eh?

So, up the beach they ambles and finds a trail *sorta* like the one they come down, except now it's a scramble up through bushes heavy with plump black brambles and apple trees just begging to be scrumped. And at t'other end of it, the road along the coast's still there, but instead of tarmac now, why, it's gold bricks for cobbles, and there's benches along it like some seaside promenade. Seems a fair bet that if this dreamland's copying the roads of the Skye they come from, it's maybe's copying towns too, so off they heads south, for Portree.

– Foxtrot, calls Lily as she bounces back from hobnobbing in fluent Eep with some otters, them having been *ebubbliant* to meet their chieftain. She scoots a spiral up one of them coin-operated telescope thingies what's dotted all along the road.

– I'm not sure Somewhere Safe is safe after all, says she. The otters say... there's something odd going on on Raaarrrrsay.

With a little jimmying to get coins for it, and jockeying for turns, they ascertains – *lemme see!* – why, is that a boat being built on the shore of the isle facing em? And the builders – *gerroff!* – is that...?

It's elves! And not yer good elves neither, as is pointy-eared pint-size imps happy to sit up trees and sing songs. No, scamps, these fuckers is all tall and haughty, pale as death in skin and hair. Surely the kind of elf what's full of pomp and piffle of his noble forebears' valiant deeds, proud of his Pure Elven Blood™, yer high and mighty scion of his ancient race of *blah blah wanky fucking blah*.

Yer fuckin racist royalist Baron Blowhard von Galahadrialarse, Ubergruppenfuhrer of the Teutonic Erl-Knights elves is what *these* are.

They's fucking *Nazi* elves!

• 2

So they gets a move on now, cause Peter minds that bollocking he overheard, and Foxy figgers they've only gone and brung over them captive spies with em – and fuck knows, maybe's *all* the groanhuffs and twerps on Skye. So they might well have a whole lot of 'splaining to do, even *warning* if Keen and Able don't know of it already. Ain't but a pinch of wishsnuff each left, but they agrees it's called for, so off they zooms, like a squadron of Spitfires, speeding south, till eventually they comes to the sign what says, *Welcome to Dun Tarakin.*

Now, it's a right queer sight as greets em in Dun Tarakin, cause in the outskirts it's all treehouses they's flying by, and as they hits the town proper, why, there's giant doll's houses with walls left open, and streets of wendy houses of all colours, blanket forts and wigwams (which Lily says is *aktcherly* called tipis) and even cottages made of boiled sugar sweeties. It looks a right funland! Oh, but there's summat worrisome about it too, scamps, cause all through the streets is Scruffians froze in place, like statues, froze mid-stride as if legging it from summat.

They don't look scared or nuffink, our heroes finds when they lands to nosey. Them hellions with their cat's eyes and batwings and suchlike all looks quite chipper. And they ain't turned to *literal* stone. But they ain't moving a muscle nor making a peep, even when's yer pokes em. Except maybe's, they thinks,

51

maybe's this girl's eyes seemed to flick at em as they passed, then suddenly forward again, like as she'd *tried* not to look but *oops*. So they works their way in past em, toward whatever's they's running from, and eventually they finds emselves at the harbour.

It's a real statue, turns out, at the end of the pier. *Nod and the Doggedy*, the plaque calls it. And there's Keen with his face hid in his hood, cauldron at his feet, harp under one arm, and a croquet mallet slung over his shoulder – what's surely from him giving dreaming scruffs all the grubbing and grooving and gaming they could wish for, eh. And there's Able riding a big Irish wolfhound what's leaping so's he can catch a ball in a hand made of silver, no less.

But there ain't sight nor sound of yer actual Scruffian gods.

• **3**

So Foxy and Squirlet's debating the Situation as they's having a sortie round this eerie scene of frozen scruffs, when Janie tugs on Flashjack's sleeve, and he ganders, pipes up, cause it's one of their crib-mates, innit:

– Firepot! Foxy, lookit: it's Firepot!

Now Firepot don't mind this, cause she were dreaming at the time, natch, but he pokes at her, gets a hint of glare, so he pokes again.

– Whatcha doing, Firepot?

– Sssshhhh! she whispers out the side of her mush, not moving her lips. Why ain't yer playing the Game?

– What game? says Foxtrot.

– *The Game*, she whispers.

And she whispers em all ventriloquistically like, how's one day yonks ago – maybe's a *thousand* yonks ago – this hellion shows up, tall as a scofflaw and voice so deep yer'd swear he were a groanhhuff... if he hadn't tweaked himself a lion's head. Anyways, he offers Keen and Able to be It in a game of Hide-and-Seek, only they hid so well they ain't been seen since. Got right boring without em, so he suggested a game of *Statues*, only when he done Eeny Meeny, it were Nuff picked as It –

– NUFF'S HERE?! says Squirlet and Foxtrot together.

– Nuff's *everywhere*, says she, ominypresents. Watching over us always. Makes the Game right hard, cause nobody can move to tag him or get In Den One Two Three until he isn't looking, can they? And if Nuff's ominypresents, that means he's never *not* looking. So that hellion said, anyway. Also he's invisible, so you can't tell. So we've been here *forever* now. I'm bursting for a pee.

– There ain't nobody watching yer, says Flashjack, least of all Nuffinmuch O'Anyfink. That's bonkers.

– Is not. That hellion said –

– That fucker was telling big fat porkies. It's Nuffinkatall Diddlysquat watching yer more like.

– Who's Nuff? says Lily.

– Boss of Bosses before Foxtrot, says Squirlet. Gone Offsky centuries ago. And I doubt it was to the Land of Nod.

– You can't say that, whispers Firepot. He can hear everything too, and just cause he's invisible now, don't mean he doesn't have feelings. He'll get offended if you go round –

– Fuck's sake, snaps Squirlet.

– We'd all dearly like Nuff back, says Foxtrot gently, but alas...

Firepot harrumphs and crosses her arms.

– He's here, she says. He – *arse!* You've got me Out now.

And just like that, Firepot goes pop like a bubble bursting and vanishes.

• 4

Well, Foxtrot tries to get more skinny on this *so-called hellion* from other frozen scruffs, but they's all taking the Game right serious. Squirlet tries snapping her fingers in this one's face. Flashjack tries tickling another. Janie even sticks a licked finger in one's ear and pushes till he falls over. But all they gets is blank stares, a blink, a muffled giggle and an *Oi!* the last three of which all ends in swearing and pops cause them scruffs, Foxtrot deductivises, is convinced they's been put Out of the Game by an imaginary Nuff, so they's woken up.

Oh, it's a right wicked scheme this Blackstone's connived – cause it ain't hard to figger how's that lionheaded liar ain't hellion at all but infuckingdubitably that Nazi cuntfucker, who's only been whisked off by yer winds of time to arrive some dark winter night a thousand yonks before em. And with the land's rightful ringleaders hoodwinked into hiding, and its hellion guards hornswoggled with a warpy lie, why, the whole Land of Somewhere Safe is *anything but* safe. It's defenceless, scamps! There's Nazi elves preparing an invasion, and if any scruff so much as blinks in peeve they'll just pop.

***

– If this Keen and Able, says Peter, are the rightful kings –
  – Ringleaders, says Squirlet.
– won't they return to save the kingdom –
  – Anarchist collective, says Foxtrot.
– in its hour of need?
  – Yer underestimating a Scruffian's commitment to shenanigans, mate, says Flashjack.
  – They'll stay hidden, says Foxy, unless –
  – *Shusht*, says Squirlet.
Furrowy browed, she leans over them maps, paperweighted by gold cobbles on the roundabout, circling her finger over peninsulas what's now going by the more Scruffian monickers of Grotternish, Snotternish, Doozynish, Monkeynish, Strathweird and Slide.
  – There.
Her finger stabs. Dun Scaith. Or as it's monickered now...
  – Fortress. Of. Shadows, reads Lily.

With the sun now setting though, scamps, and no wishsnuff for flying, an umpty-plonk mile hike in darkness don't seem the savviest move, especially not with that lionheaded Nazi fucker lurking out there somewheres, maybe's his Addanc too – *that horrid thing that scrobbled Peter*, says Lily, and sheepish Peter don't correct her how, um, it was more a *nobbling* than a *scrobbling*, really. So, for a temporary crib, they claims a nice gingerbread house with spiky icing for its painted pebbledash, and after a fine feast on the furniture, they snuggles down to sleep in the softest muffiny beds.

• 5

What with a good night's kip and a breakfast of pure sugar rush, they's all in fine fettle when they sets out the next morn. A thousand yonks since him arriving, maybe's Blackstone's just pegged it, as groanhuffs tends to. And why, even if Keen and Able ain't hid in that Fortress of Shadows, it *has* to be a good place to stash the Stamp and dig in against invading Nazis, innit. So they's whistling merrily as they marches south into thick forest.
  Ain't until *well* after midday they starts arguing over whether they's missed that *really important* left turn.

– It's the River Slickyhand, says Squirlet.
  – It can't be, says Foxtrot. My calculations –

– must be wrong.

– Well, did *you* see sóme hidden turn-off?

– Oh, so it's *my* fault?

Trailing along a safe ways behind, the others keeps quieter'n a pack of sprogs in back of a Volkswagon headed for a caravan holiday in Cornwall what's ended up in Wales, mum and dad at snippy loggerheads. It don't exactly help that there's an enormous rook circling in the sky, and Flashjack's *sure* he clocked a wolf in the underbrush, keeping pace. Carrion animals following em. No, that ain't *awfully* reassuring.

It's only befitting, really, them being lost, when's they finds emselves in the Valley of Lost Things, stumbling out of an holloway onto the shores of what *might* be Loch Duff, (says Peter helpfully, peeping between bonces at the map, getting shrivelling scowls for it,) into a veritable *midden* of Very Important Thingamajigs – great dunes of ration books, keys, spectacles, diaries, even a rag Lily unwraps to find...

– Ewww! she says. Whoever should want to keep a mouldy old crust of bread?

– Considering why one would hide that, says Foxtrot, it's probably the most valuable thing here.

– Oh, says Lily.

They's pushed on through more wildwoods, to the shores of what *might* be Loch Ethane, (Peter *don't* say) when, with evenfall, it's decided to camp – for a nosh and kip, eh? So, as Flashjack sets to guddling a fish, Foxtrot slinks off into the forest, returning presently with a wee white rabbit in a pocketwatched waistcoat, garotte round its throat. He's just skinning it for the fire when an almighty CRACK! sends em racing for the source: Lily's rifle! Lily!

Yeah, Lily standing proud over a dead unicorn.

– Perhaps... a trifle more meat than required? says Foxy.

– Pemmican? says Lily.

• 6

Now, I *suppose* Foxtrot might've minded them twerps becoming midges, and it's *conceivable* he overheard that rabbit muttering about being late in a most *groanhuffy* punctiliousness regarding punctuality, but, look, *they* wasn't to know it were groanhuff's dreamselves they was scoffing, and it were *probably* just sleeping groanhuffs, not locals what'd been transported and transformogrificated. So we needn't count it as cannibalism, *strictly speaking*.

Besides, it were in a good cause, as them six woke up the next morn feeling much less conniptious and crotchety, rallied and ready to sort out where the fuck they was and where's to go.

So now Peter braves to suggest this must be Loch Ethane, and these hills around em the Cool'uns, why, they must be halfways into Strathweird. And Foxtrot concedes as how maybe's the Land of Nod might've flouted his calculations of distance by sun angles and strides. And Squirlet allows as how maybe's the Land of Somewhere Safe might've hid that turn to be took even from her. But not to fuss, they agrees. They *could* keep heading south to the coast, take the long way round, *or* cut east over the hills to this here inlet, where Strathweird meets Slide.

South seems the safest route – for all of half an hour before's they's galumphed into schlurping marsh, footstuck and sunkslogging, eventually having to heave Janiemalinky's longpins free and all ending up in a great floppety splat of a heap, flailing and filthed.
    – Fuck this to fucking fuck, says Flashjack.
    – Oh, this is the parson's pickle, says Peter. The perfect parson's pickle! I shan't go a step further!
    And they all agrees he has a point, eh, it'd be crackers trudging on through this, so it's a sharp left and onward, upward, Squirlet ahead, peepers peeled for a sneaky mountain pass.

All day they treks and scrambles, stinked with sludge and slickery with sweat, clambering up and up by corries and ridges, to the very peak of Mount Blabbing, scamps, the very peak. It's a well weary bunch as comes plodding down t'other side, following a trickle as becomes a burn as becomes a cascade as becomes, oh, the flabbergasting phantasmagnificent Dunachin Falls they stands beneath, scamps, in its thundering steamy spray, gobsmacked. Because that water...
    – It's hot, says Lily. It's a hot waterfall.
    – A hotterfall! says Peter.
    So, showered, soothed, they's lazing peaches-and-creamy *dreamy* when's the centaurs attack.

• 7

– Well, if it's not one thing, it's another, says Peter.
    Hands and feet lashed, plonked across a centaur's back, he looks down at Lily bouncing in her net – looking jolly well peeved too.

– Bloody groanhuffs, she grumps. What chance is there against Adolf when your own Allies scrobble you?

He can't argue. For all's their mythicality, their brawny human uppers and horsie bodies, brown-flanked with great white fluffy feathering on their fetlocks like Clydesdales, well, the khaki canvass saddlebags, helmets and Lee Enfields slung over shoulders instead of quivers *are* summat of a giveaway. Also the prattling in Polish.

Led into the great stone fort of Dun Winkle overlooking Loch Slappy, Foxtrot still trying to wheedle em mulish centaurs – *vital mission, old boy, really, we've no time for this delay* – the Situation don't get any more auspicious in terms of them groanhuffs as ought to be *helping* our heroes even so much as not being a bleeding hindrance, cause their Commanding Officer, sat up on his stone throne, is a Sir Godfrey whose literal snorty bullheadedness is... most likely not a good sign. And true to form:

– Nazi elves? says this minotaur to Foxy. Pishposh and balderdash, boy! Balderdash!

– No, children, says he, there's a greater threat by far, I say. A ruddy dragon, what!

Lily and Peter looks at each other, then at the two cheery satyrs, one bepectacled and one beer-bellied, what Sir Godfrey has at least been foxtrotted into dispatching by motorbike and sidecar up to Dun Tarakin for a sortie. He couldn't possibly, he blusters, spare another soul on such rumours though – rumours! Gossip and tittle-tattle! There's a *dragon* abroad, what!

– A dragon? whispers Lily. Really?
– Tell the truth, whispers Tubbs, I think he's gone a bit barmy.
– Bonkers even, whispers Goggles.
– Doolally.

– It's not an *unmitigated* disaster, says Foxtrot as the wee steamboat flotilla putters over Loch Slappy.

– We're on a dragon hunt, says Squirlet. With a monomaniac minotaur.
– I have a plan.
– I hope it don't involve slaying any dragons, says Flashjack. Just cause yer burns some shit down, don't make yer a monster.
– It'll be fine, old boy. I doubt we'll even *see* a dragon.
– I should feel quite miffed if *I* were hunted, says Lily.
– We won't even be *on* the hunt.

— The rifles don't seem very sporting, says Peter.

— Look, we're *only here for the boat*, says Foxtrot.

• **8**

So the burning boat goes BOOM! just a little laters, down in the loch, and through the 'splosion of flames as makes Flashjack's eyes go wider than the sight of his Puckerscruff's pert tush comes the bloody great flying lizard that weren't quite as much, as it turns out, the figment of Sir Godfrey's imagination as Foxtrot anticipated. Shrieking and soaring in it comes, for another dive at the chaos of rearing centaurs all stuck in the gorge what cuts in from the beach to its cave. At the mouth of which, Sir Godfrey's remains is smelling right roast beefy.

— Nice plan, mutters Squirlet, somewhere's under the crush of em all crammed into a nook betwixt the biggest rocks to hand, ducked down from the centaurs' gunfire and the cricket ball globs of napalm death now strafing the shingle of fancy silverware as is the dragon's hoard. Again. So, no. With that gorge being but a narrow gouge in the shorefront cliffs, they didn't *quite* get the chance to dawdle behind, sneakily circle back, nick a boat, and offsky for Dun Scaith. And, yeah, with its sides being thirty foot high and sheer, they might be a bit trapped now.

— Yer an SS Jaguar 100 in the skies! roars Flashjack, stood up with his arms outstretched in adoration. A Triumph Tiger T100 with wings! Oh, lookit him, Foxy! Squirlet, just lookit that gorgeous beast!

Fireballs pounding the beach in a beeline their way, eight hands and two otter paws drags Flashjack back down just as the dragon swooshes overhead and into a sharp turn straight up, corkscrewing in the air so's its blue underbelly and green back flashes in the sunlight, before it's turned, poised in the air, then diving again, roaring.

— I'm going to call him Spitfire, croons Flashjack.

— Run! Now!

On the loch, them routed centaurs is back on the last steamboats, hightailing it, and with the dragon after em, it's our heroes' break. A crevice clocked by Squirlet! They sprints, scrabbles, squidgeting emselves up, nimble Lily first, then... Clambering onto the clifftop, leaping atop an outcrop, right hand raised in Victory V-sign, whole sodding fist afire like a flaming torch, Flashjack roars.

— Burn, baby, burn!

The dragon turns, sees, comes rocketing toward em — *Flashjack! You*

58

fucking – only to slam to an halt before the scallywag, pinions pounding air. And it raises its head, roars exultation back.

• 9

Oh, but, scamps – just when's it seems bonce-bogglingly *okay*, just when's Lily and Peter is stood jawdropped at the sight of the scallywag up on his peak of precipice, so wild and fiery the fucking *dragon* beating its wings in the air beyond knows him for a kindred soul, just when's Foxtrot and Squirlet is goggling speechless at their impetuous hellion's bloody unbossable recklessness *not* aktcherly getting em all barbecued... then, scamps, then, it's Janiemalinky Longpins humphs the rucksack with the Stamp up onto that clifftop, and hauls herself up to stand.

In the shining armour of a knight.

It's Peter who sees it coming, Peter who hurls himself at Janie – *Look out!* – her head still only half-up as she rises. Peter who slams cannonball into her and knocks her flat – near sends em both over the edge, by fuck, back down into the gorge, but saves her, scamps, from a flame-grilling he don't even stop to think might not kill her. Would that dragonfire melt armour, scour her Stamp right off? Or would the charred cinder of her just scream till she's sprung back? He don't fucking care, scamps, just slams her from the fireball's path.

It's Lily who dives to another angle of support for these scruffs they's fallen in with, Lily who don't stop to think how's she don't owe them scruffs nuffink, Lily who just acts on her instincts as the stray she surely is, to defend her new crib mates, to mind their backs, to fight. Lily who rolls and dives for her sharpshooter's rifle, and brings it up to her shoulder, that Springfield Trapdoor, with the barrel pointing straight at the dragon's head now, even as Flashjack's throwing a palm out each way to halt the calamity, screaming at em:
– Nooooooo!

Oh, and he spins, that scallywag, in a lightning blur, one hand reaching for the bullet, the other for the fireball, like as he might catch em, pluck em out of the very air. He spins so fast yer has to slow it down to even imagine it, him twirling as the hot lead goes by him on one side and the fiery spitball goes by on the other. And he almost does it, scamps, almost. His fingertips fucking well *taps* that bullet as it passes. His palm fucking *grazes* the fireball. But it ain't enough, scamps. Not for one.

• 10

– Oh, fly, boy, fly, sobs Flashjack. I'll help yer burn every fucking toff in his Tin Man suit to a bleeding crisp, nick yer every silver spoon from every stately home in all of Old Blighty, if yer just flies like the fucking clappers for us, mate.

Astraddle the dragon's shoulders, hunched over to cling to its neck with one hand and cradle Lily's blackburnt form in the crook of his other arm, he urges Spitfire onward with every breath. It weren't the dragon's fault. He weren't to know. It were Flashjack fucked up. Oh, for once he shoulda thunk.

A scamp and a scrag clamped in the talons of his forefeet, stray and scofflaw clasped in his hindfeet, Spitfire is heavy in the air, burdened beyond his sleek fighter's build, but he hammers it hard, scamps, low over water darkening with dusk, over ripples reflecting the deep blue sky. He hammers it hard for the coast of Slide, for the castle of Dun Scaith, perched there on a plug of basalt as is an isle at high tide, cut off from the mainland moors but for the stone arches of support for its drawbridge. For Lily's life, Spitfire flies.

– Fuck off! Flashjack shouts at the ginormous raven what seems to be follering em over the loch. Fuck the fuck off! he shouts, twisting to fire a warning shot from his highwayman's flintlock. Yer ain't having her!

Oh, Keen and Able *has* to be at Dun Scaith, eh, scamps? They *has* to be hid in that Fortress of Shadows: Keen, Dinguses, Baccy, first and fiercest of all tweaked to hellion, who'll grin to the scallywag's defiance of death; Able, sweet Apple, soft Pillow, Keen's gentle brother, who'll pity the poor stray. Oh, they'll can make-believe Lily healed, for sure.

So Spitfire flies.

So you listen, scamps. There might's be *metaphorical* dragons what raids villages and eats virgins, but the truth behind em's *pogroms and crusades*, mate; it's the fuckin *knights,* raiding and claiming they's hunting monsters – as we's their hunted monsters now, huddled here tonight. So don't you believe a word from em groanhuff cuntfuckers when's they projectifies their *own* crimes on some innocent beastie like Spitfire as only ever nicked the odd dinner set, torched a manor house or three.

No, scamps, that Spitfire struck back at his attackers, but gentled and friended by Flashjack...?

How he flies!

Part Six

• 1

Meanwhiles, scamps...

On the battlement of her great tower, she stands, the Scáthach, the *Shadow*, as give that castle its name, the Warrior Maid as taught Cuchullain himself to fight, even give him his mighty barbed spear. On the battlements of her great keep, where's once that Faerie Flag flew high, where's once she brung her fierce-Fixed kin fallen in battle, dreaming in delirium as they slipped toward death, and cried out, *Turn and knock!* and as they did so, oh, the Land of Somewhere Safe were opened to them.

Oh, them were the days, a thousand yonks ago!

Ferocious gaze fixed to the west, on the setting sun and the dragon rushing in out of it, on the scruffs and strays that dragon carries, on the magics *they* carries, in an empty wishsnuff tin, in a Silver Chanter and a Silver Cloak, in the very Stamp itself – cause she can smell the wishsnuff and the cloak, hear the chanter's whistle, feel the Stamp upon her chest – she stands, craned forward over the parapet's edge, every inch of her singing: *Come on!* For she can *taste* the terrible acrid burning pain of a stray struck down in valiant fight.

To her belt goes her hand, to the two great horns what Keen hacked off so's to hide himself. Not to the left horn though, no, scamps, for that's only to be blown in times of battle, to summon Keen's each-uisge, his kelpie cavalry, the wild horses from the waves what drags invaders to their death. That's only for a scruff to use, and only one them kelpies deems wild enough to follow.

61

No, it's the right horn she grabs, scamps, as will heal any what sips from it.
– To me, laddie! To me! she cries. Throw her down!

And Spitfire's turning the tightest spiral dragon ever turned, to hang in the air above the tower, so's all's em kids carried by him can see her stood there in her crow-feather cloak, a Rake who took the Stamp long afore Ripper Vicky's Empire, afore even the Children's Crusade, who took the name Erin O'Morrigan after a life of battles she'd have no more of, mistakes she'd never make again. They sees her face, and Flashjack just knows to trust; he's tossing Lily down to be caught in a flourish of cloak even as Peter cries out:
– Lady Fay!

• 2

With Foxtrot and Squirlet dropped to roll like paratroopers, Peter and Janie dumped to stumble and stagger, Flashjack somersaulting to land in a crouch, they all comes haring across the tower's flat roof to where's that Rake cradles Lily in her lap to gloogle whisky from a hipflask into the horn, tip a sip of it between the lips of an otter so awful burned, scamps, oh, yer wouldn't hardly imagine it *possible* she still lived. But glory be, ickle ones, glory be! Live she did, and live she would, the whole horror of her healing before their very eyes.

They gawps as silver fur springs back, as Lily gasps – *the Stamp!* – gawps more as that Rake... boops Lily's snoot with a knuckle and the cloak unfurls, limbs, bod and bonce all popping back to scampsize – *Well, I never!* – but Erin O'Morrigan ain't any less indomitable than Lady Fay. With a flurry, she's swooping em up:
– Well, come ye in, bairns! Well met and welcome! Ye've kept the Stamp safe, lassie? And my Flag? Grand, grand!
And in a dervishy whirl, they's downstairs – *Sit! Sit!* – at a fingerclicked feast.
– Tuck in!
And as they does... She fabbles of this land.

It were one Rammarty Joe, she says as they chomps, brung the Stamp to Albion's isles, asking sanctuary from the savage locals, Fumers by name. A good Rake he were, but Fixed browbeaten, broken, so when he warns against abusing the Stamp, them Fumers just laughs and nabs it, starts Fixing themselves, tweaking themselves to giants. Then Fixes some slaves, naturally, to serve em. Scruffians and Rakes of days of yore.

Dunnians they was dubbed, for the muck they was held as, the forts they was held in, but just like their laters, they resisted... rebelled.

And, oh, they *dreamt*.

Twas a sore comeuppance them Fumers met, at the hands of an hellion tribe sprung roaring from nightmares, led by Nod and the Doggedy – Able and Keen – with Lookit McKeen Longhand as them brothers' champion, ringleader of all rammies. Weren't no battle ever won against Lookit's Lance, his crew of warriors so bloodthirsty only opium pounded from poppy seeds could calm em. Wild and free, they was, scamps, halfways in the Land of Nod, fed from the Doggedy's Cauldron, and the world lit afire for em with the burning sword of a truth none can escape and none resist: freedom.

• 3

She's afire herself as she fabbles it, scamps, oh, cause if Lookit were the *hero* of them ancient Scruffians' rebellions, the Morrigan were a *nemesis* sprung from the darker wilds of Rakes' revenges. At the head of her table in the Great Hall she sits, as they tears into chicken drumsticks and strips hambones, munches sausages, and it's halfways the fire in her eyes lighting it all, as it's that in the hearth, or the torches on the walls. But they can see the Shadow in her too, the flicker of dark, as she comes to how this Appleland fell.

For hundreds of yonks, see, theirs were the dream keeping Albion just. Every Boss of every gingery Scot, black Irish or bastard British whatever, every Boudicca or Arthur, weren't *none* of em some *king* or *queen*, but just a chief as earned election by savvy and spunk. And had it validated by what's *they* called the Stone of Feels, the Stone of Skins... the Stone of Destiny. To Appleland, they'd all come, to have the Stamp read em, so's the truth of em could be noseyed upon it, that stone singing out how honourable they was – or not.

But then...

Called himself Saint Mithras, he did, the one who came, perhaps some thousand yonks ago, perhaps yesterday, with a glamour of lies befuddling the very history of the land.

See, scamps, when yer groanhuff dreams themself as white rabbit, or fish, or unicorn, they ain't surprised at that, is they? Yer's had such dreams yerselves, eh, where's yer memories shifts to fit actions, where's even from one tick to the next, what yer remembers happening to yer changes, rewrote like yer was tweaking yer Stamp.

Well, now the whole Land of Nod's had a thousand bleeding yonks of it rewrote.

So what she minds, as in a dream... don't quite add up: a lionheaded hellion coming ashore on a coracle, promising summat called Christmas if everyone just went to sleep; Rammarty Joe disappearing with the Stamp; Lookit gone hunting for him; Keen and Able lost in a game of Hide-and-Seek – must've hid so well, scruffs said, they forgot where they put themselves; bloody battles with comrades turned enemies, her last loyal fellows falling one by one, scrubbed; herself walking away from it all, into the waking world.

For a thousand yonks, she's lived glamoured as sundry Lady Fays.

• 4

Is that the truth of it? Well, it's the fabble of it now, says she. Part of her's sure it's wrong, that her Dunnian kin, full-grown and pint-size, roved the real world until those dreadful imperial Romans come along, that she lived in Dun Scaith on Skye through their twilight centuries, until the last Dunnian left for an Appleland where all's been *fun* these last thousand yonks, Nod and the Doggedy playing ringleaders of the revels to this day. Until...

With the young Scruffians' somewhat *rash* opening of the Bridge outside her castle's sphere of containment... something's changed.

So they tells her of Blackstone, of him being a Nazi, his transformogrication and everything.

– Ochone, ochone, says she.

Cause she's had many a fracas with that reverend in her role as Lady Fay, had to socialise with him at Soltice Ceilidhs, suffer through him waffling on about his bleeding allegorical novel with its bollocks moral of sin and salvation. She knows all about his vision of a Father's Land, purged of all darkness, decadence and deviance, open only to innocents pure as the driven snow.

He's working to turn the Land of Nod, she realises, into his Nazi Heaven.

– Oh, it's all my fault, says Peter. If I hadn't stolen the Stamp for him, he mightn't even be here.

On the battlements of Dun Scaith, he looks out over the moonlit water, feeling stupid in his silly spaceman silver, and alone as if he *were* in space. He'd shove his hands into his greatcoat pockets in a mopey hunch if he only had em.

– Och, laddie.

Erin pats his shoulder.

– Oh, he remembers.

He unzips the spacesuit to rumpage in shorts pocket and down his shirt, ferret out the wishsnuff and chanter.

– It's not the only thing I stole.

She looks sorta wistful as she turns the chanter in her fingers. It were Able's, she fabbles him. As Keen's left horn called his kelpie cavalry, so Able's pipe whistled up the wind, and his Good Ship to sail it – sunk a thousand yonks, alas, Able alone knows where.

– Och, she says, best I ever got from it's a banshee babby's squawl. Keep it. And as for the wishsnuff...

She gives the tin a wee shake, hands it back with a wink as makes him... curious. Makes him pop the lid, to find it full.

– No harm done, she says.

• 5

– No *harm done?* growls Squirlet inside, as Peter stands before them scruffs for his reckoning, Erin behind with hands gentle on his shoulders, herself having fortified him into coming clean – *Whip the plaster off and have done with it, laddie.*

– Peter, how could you? says Lily. We thought you were scrobbled and... how *could* you?

– Bad form, old boy, says Foxtrot.

Janie shakes her head.

– Well, there *were* an abominable lake monster involved, says Flashjack.

– Still, snaps Squirlet.

– Children, says Erin in a voice as reminds a scamp and scrag that even with centuries each... they's *still* nippers beside her.

So the traitor's confessed, scamps, and about time too, and with a little stern reminding of fallibilities and explifications of an Addanc's workings on the part of Erin O'Morrigan, who speaks like's she might even have firsthand experience of such cold wet clutches and the cock-ups born of em, feathers is unruffled to a range of acceptances from grudging to blithe. But yer know what, scamps? Don't mean all Peter's mope's just washed away like that. Still feels like fucking shit, mate, so he does. Not far off that Addanc being latched on his back, really.

A *perfect rotter.*

***

It's not running away though, scamps, when he takes a snort of that wishsnuff up on the battlements, in the wee hours of the morning, and flies off over the moonlit loch. No, it's just cause he can't sleep, for the peace of it, to be soaring free of the weight of himself. He don't go far, just finds himself on the cliff above Spitfire's cave, where's the dragon's snoring away. Finds Lily's ickle cowboy hat and takes it back to Dun Scaith, sets it down on a parapet. Whooshes up into the sky again, back off into the night.

He ain't running away, scamps, as he heads northish along the coast of Slide, looking over to his left at a distant speck of orangey light, what's maybe's them centaurs in Dun Winkle, eh, however many's left of em, drinking toasts around the fire to their roasted CO, whether in good riddance or respect. He's just flying aimless, really, until that light minds him of two Home Guard satyrs sent to investergate the scruffs' stories of Nazi elves prepping an invasion of Dun Tarakin. It's only then he thinks... maybe's he could do some recon himself. And off he goes.

• 6

It's a gryphon as delivers Peter's spaceman suit with the reverend's message, the next morn after lunch, as the War Meeting's in full flow as to how to deal with the invasion threat, and the blackguardry of Blackstone wherever he might be, and whatever the fuck's befallen Peter – with Squirlet, for all's her being the toughest nut, being the stubbornest in reckoning foul play over flight. It's a gryphon's screech brings em all rushing to the drawbridge – and fitting that is, yer lion and eagle the most regal of beasts, beloveds of every imperial fuck from Nero to the Nazis.

– I ain't staying behind, says Flashjack. There's a Liberating needing done, mate.
   – Look, it's only sensible, says Foxtrot. It's what you're here for.
   – Janie stays here with the Stamp, says Squirlet. So her *hellion escort* stays with her.
   Janie steps up beside Flashjack, arms folded: *nope.*
   – Oh, *come on,* says Squirlet.
   Thing is, for all's Foxtrot's and Squirlet's centuries of savvy, scruffs isn't *really* bossable when push comes to shove, just easy-oasy when it don't. And as much as Peter done em wrong, now's he's Gone Offsky and got himself scrobbled...

Well, there ain't nuffink more stray than that.

As the Morrigan's bloodcurdling howl dies down, the four scruffs wiggles fingers in ears, and Lily unclaps her paws from her own.

– Was that absolutely necessary? says Foxtrot.

– Rallying the troops, laddie, says Erin. What's the loyalest beast?

– Dog, says Flashjack. Duh.

– And what does a dog dream themself, lad?

And first they hears the howling, then they sees em come, racing in over the moors, great hoary brutes. Queerly, the biggest of all, clear leader of the pack, has a right lollopy look and stride, like's he ain't even full-growed yet. More a *whelp* than an *adult* wolf.

As Flashjack, tongue and teeth marking his kinship, bounds around beyond the drawbridge, bonding with these lupine allies, he's too busy to even notice the ginormous raven he swore bloody murder at from his other beastly instamate, flying in now from the west, smaller ones joining it from all directions.

– More allies? says Squirlet.

– Might not mind their own names, lass, but I'd trust their mettle with my skin. And they might be too grown and grim to *play* here as you scruffs... but a Rake still dreams.

That's right, scamp. Bang on! What *else* would Rakes be but rooks?

• 7

– Does that mean, says Lily, we were eating... oh, I feel rather queasy.

– Best not to think of it, says Foxtrot.

In the raven-drawn chariot of Erin O'Morrigan, they ride, in her sleek black beast of a chariot as might, in another world, look more'n a bit Bentleyish, wolves racing below, and oh, however's that lolloping lupine leader keeps pace, fuck knows, scamps, cause they's bloody *bombing* it over the moors of Slide, up and around, along the coast looking out on Scalp Isle, through the Cool'uns, and over Slickyhand, up past Dun Tarakin...

To the Stour and winter.

It's a stark land they enters, all em apple trees stripped to tawny gorse and grim rock along a gold-cobbled road now grey. Where's the Grotternish they arrived in were a dream of Skye so foresty they didn't even *see* the precipice and pinnacles they passed, now as they comes in over the loch-split lowland nooked betwixt scarp's edge and sea, yer couldn't miss the Old Man jutting from the snowpatched hillside. Or how's befront the monstrous bluff looming behind it, a mountainous outcrop's now a carved triangular pediment over a monumental entrance, like some temple or tomb.

As they circles the Old Man widdershins, descending to the base of that monolith's grassy mound of pedestal, to where's that slope meets a flat field of solid ice, as they sees the ice steps leading up from there to a cavernous maw now cut into the cliff-face... Now, scamps, from between the pillars each side carved as Teutonic Knights in sword arch salute, out of shadows aflicker with torchlight, comes Blackstone, His Leonine Majesty, striding proud with a retinue of deathly pale Aryan catwalk nobs dressed in yer finest Hugo Boss.

And Peter shivering in tanktop and shorts.

– Dear children, says that Nazi fuck – voice deeper now with liony rumbling. And Lady Fay, *of course*.

Gathered at their backs, an army of wolves rumbles deeper.

– It is my privilege to return your comrade.

And with none more shocked than Peter, he shoves the boy out onto the ice, to slip, and scramble, and scurry into hearty embraces – *Peter! Old boy! Yer okay!*

– It is my pleasure, says Blackstone, to see a *traitor* returned to meet justice.

– Justice? growls Erin.

And if ever a lion could smirk.

– Under the Law of the Land, he roars. THE TRAITOR MUST DIE!

• 8

In blackening skies, thunder rumbles, scamps, over a scene of parlay to chill the blood. Picture it: this great rink of ice, and faced-off across it: our heroes with an army of wolves and ravens at their back, a veritable goddess of war in front; that lionheaded usurper with his honour guard of Nazi elves *well* outnumbered... but with this towering lowering *edifice* of stony majesty behind him.

– THE LAW OF THE LAND! he bellows, and thunder rolls. I was there when it was written –

– Not the first time round, says Erin.

– Defy it, he gloats. And be *exiled*.

The War Meeting is... vigorously opinionated.

– Fuck yer Law of the Land, says Flashjack. Pile of fucking wank.

– Damn straight, mutters Squirlet. Since when would Keen and Able have *laws* –?

– It's not so simple, says Foxtrot and Erin together.

They looks at each other. Erin flourishes an hand: *Go on.*

– It's a Game, he says. Like the *Statues* game, Firepot in Dun Tarakin. Break the rules and... *Pop.*

– We're all Out, says Peter. And none left to stop him. Oh, that's *diabolical.*

– Despicable, says Lily.

– I shan't be his blasted pawn again, says Peter. Not in this. I bloody shan't!

– It won't work, says Foxtrot pacing. Think about it.

– A Rake's life for a mortal bairn's, laddie, says Erin. He'll no can resist it.

– And the Queen of the Dead dies for a sinner's life, he says. Heathen forces vanquished, sacrifice, salvation. Think.

The horror dawns.

– A *Christian allegory*, shudders Erin.

– A Christian allegory, says Foxtrot. Written into the Land of Nod.

– Oh, it's the Devil and the deep blue sea, says Lily. Whatever can we –?

– Stop, says Peter quietly. Just *stop.*

And they stops at his tone, so sure in its calm, resolute.

– The traitor must die, he says.

– Yer wants yer bonce looked at, says Flashjack. Did yer blow yer nose fifty feet up and plop down arse-upwards or summat? Yer's gone crackers, mate.

– You mustn't, Peter, says Lily. Foxtrot, tell him he mustn't.

– There's every chance this is a winning strategy for him too, says Foxtrot. If we play his Game –

Janie tugs at Foxtrot's sleeve.

– At least you won't be Out, says Peter, and the Land won't be... *allegorified.*

Janie jiggles Foxtrot's arm.

– Just let me think, old boy, I'm sure... *What?*

Janie unslings the rucksack from her back, flaps an hand flat, like: *duh.*

• 9

Weren't none of them scruffs a fabbler like yours truly, scamps, to do it proper like, with the full fabbling of *The Taking of the Stamp* we gives strays before's joining, so's they knows the score. But between them four – with even Janie contributing the odd pokey mimey reminder of some bit they'd skipped – between em, they gots the *gist* of it across. Then they gots Peter lain on the ground, shirt open and belt betwixt teeth, and they rolled the Stamp upways over his chest to read him, downways to write, to Fix him.

And the scrag rose, ready.

It's Squirlet takes him first for training, a quick crash course in how to hide whatevers, not the chanter or the wishsnuff maybe's – they's too big – but at least a wee shiv, hid where's Blackstone will never find it. And she learns him how to hide himself in shadows in an empty room, so's he can sneak away afterwards, like.

See, if Peter's to be hung, or shot blindfolded against a wall, or whatever, it ain't to be the scruffs doing it. No, they *could* do it that way with the fucker just watching, but this is... an opportunity, innit.

It's Foxtrot takes him next, gives him all the centuries of savvy he can cram into one hour: how to escape shackles, pick a lock, clear a drugged mind, even focus it to figger a Dire Situation, to plot a path from predicament to objective. To execute a perfect assassination. However's Peter springs back, in whatever pickle, the cunning Foxy plots him a plan for it.

See, if they just *bows* to His Nibs's almighty authority, just *submits* to his Law, well, Blackstone can take all that tedious *responsibility* off their hands, eh. And bring Scruffian vengeance into his lair.

So, after a last round of edification from Flashjack in yer more physical side of being Scruffian, the scrag looks round his crib-mates one by one and –

– Wait, says Lily. If it isn't *awfully* forward... I think *I* should very much like...

– Yer in, nods Flashjack.

So she unfurls her otter cloak, what she'd put back on, seeing as her rifle (and cowboy hat) weren't best sized to her human form, (and because, truth be told, she'd aktcherly got to kinda like being an otter.)

– I don't *mind* it, says she, but I'd rather not risk being *Fixed* so.

• 10

So it's long past a nightfall come early in the Land of Nod, in this wintry foothold of Blackstone's bastard combo of fascism and so-called Christianity. It's dark and bitter cold as befits the coming birthday not of yer *actual* Joshyer Cripes – bless his ickle anarchosocialist socks – no, but of that lionheaded god them Roman Emperors swapped in, with lies of blood sacrifice washing wickedry away, Bob's yer uncle, like's yer fuck-ups was stains to be wiped off for yer *own* good, not hurts done to others yer just *makes up for* and *don't fucking do again*, duh.

It's dark and bitter cold as the six scruffs steps out onto the ice, and calls Blackstone out from his Chapel Pitiless, as they lays down their weapons and kneels, and Peter walks forward to be taken into the charge of Saint Mithras, as a penitent sinner – who ain't fucking well having anyone else, mortal or magical, die in his place, ta much. And up them icy steps he goes, between them proud pillars of Baron von Crusade and Archduke Pogrom, into the torchlit hollows echoing with pious chants of *Herr Fuhrer, who art in Heaven, hallowed be thy name.*

Oh, scamps, since Orphan's trip to Hades to sing for the Lord of the Dead and win a princess back, since that first Scruffian the Stamp were made for, so's his mission wouldn't wash away in the Lethe, scamps, ain't none suffered so much as Peter did then, stripped and whipped till's the blood and his ickle horns made him the very spit of the Devil, his heart cut out for being heartless, his guts spilled out for being gutless – and he hadn't no backbone nor balls, says this Lion of Judgement, so *they'd* to go too.

Oh, pitiable Peter!

But we won't dawdle and dwell on it, scamps, as some awesome act of sacrifice averting yer archvillain's triumph over's an earthly paradise turned to shit by lies. Cause it fucking *weren't*. For them scruffs it were just a ruse getting Peter into position, a gruesome horror, but one as'd be undone – well, except for the PTSD – with Peter springing back. And any other ways yer looks at it, what ain't a sadist or saint's psycho excuses, it were just a usurping motherfucker torturing his *dear child.*

Well, not *just* that. Not when them bells began tolling Blackstone's Midnight Mass.

Part Seven

• 1

Now, scamps, yer's maybe heard one groanhuff's botching of our fabbling craft what tells of a magical nowhereland island, and a flying kiddo as plays there and don't never grow up – never never! And yer might have heard a whole *classical mythology* of groanhuff's flubbings of the fabbling art what includes this kiddyish god with ickle pointy horns on his bonce what lives out in the forest tootling on his pipe. Sounds kinda Petery, eh? And where's both yer flighty nowhereland scrag and yer flutey horny hellion is called *Pan*, that might's strike yer as summat of a suspicious coincidence.

Well, see, them bells rang out across the whole land, and as oughts to be clear from that rewritten thousand yonks, if not just from yer own doolalliest dreams, time ain't exactly stable in the Land of Nod, and if yer can nip from tomorrow to last Tuesday in there, fuck knows, no reason a dream of happenings on one particklar Christmas Day couldn't be half-remembered by folk visiting from elsewhens, some Edwardian scribbler or Athenian singer who wakes back up in yesteryear with a fuzzy notion of... summat Very Important to do with a flying flutist hellion scrag.

Why, there's even one groanhuff bungling of a fabble what ain't just concocted around some fudged fancy of Peter, but 'members the whole dark deed, cause back in the year Hardly Anyfink At All AD, there's a tale tattled of these sailors who's passing an island called Peace when's they hears a voice ringing out: *Pan is dead! Great Pan is dead!*

Gob's truth! Slickspit, you look it up on yer iPhone doohickey. So you tell me if that don't prove this here fabble of The Land of Somewhere Safe is true. Independent verification, mate. Even groanhuff *history* records it!

But oh, scamps, it's a dark midnight with a message of murder clanging across this land what's meant to be a playground, cause with the turn of Christmas Eve to Christmas Day, this were the birthday of Mithras being rung out with the deathday of that hornpiping horned pagan flighty funster of the forests. Why, it's an ugly fucking flimflam *sermon* of this scruff what's half Keen, half Able, and all fucking *play* being slain on the altar of this imperialist travesty of everything Joshyer Cripes ever stood for. Glad fucking tidings, my arse...

It's a *Nazi Christmas allegory*, scamps!

• 2

When's he springs back, mind, gasping awake after hours of pain and darkness, Peter don't know diddly of this, no more'n his comrades camped out on the hillside, dug in for a siege but itching for assault. When's he jolts aware into flashbacks like he's still in the horror – wild-eyed and panting, scrabbling back against a wall until he clears his noggin, focuses as Foxtrot learnt him – he don't know why Blackstone's smirking, looking back at him from the balcony outside... some sort of bell tower he's in, it seems.

He savvies that smirk can't mean nuffink good, though.

– Come, dear child, says Blackstone. The view is quite inspiring.

As Peter edges forward, he clocks how's the balcony overlooks the Old Man. Why, they must be near enough in that monstrous pediment's point.

– Impressive, no? says Blackstone. It's said a priest once summoned the Devil himself upon it, *harnessed* him, rode the horned fiend all the way to Rome and back, to fetch the truth of when Easter should be celebrated. Ha! I rather think they've muddled Empire with Reich, *when* with *how*, and Easter with Christmas, but I do believe, dear child, you've carried my truth quite effectively.

Beyond the Old Man and the sea, beyond a mainland hazed as if behind some veil, the sky's lightening.

– A new day comes, says Blackstone. An end to Scruffian lawlessness. The ultimate new beginning.

And talk about an utter cock, scamps. The way he crows... of an end so endy, it'll reach right back to scrub the Land of Nod afore it's even begun. And in place of Somewhere Safe, it'll be his Father's Land. Imagine it, scamps: all history's enslaved scruffs never having nowhere's to escape in slumber. Think how's they'll lose hope, how many Liberatings might never happen!

— You absolute... *fucker*, blurts Peter.

Blackstone's smug liony gaze stays on that Old Man.

— A sleeping giant's thumb, he purrs. A *collossal Heathenry* sunk in slumber. Where Wickedness was harnessed, ridden by Piety to bring the Good News of Salvation. Oh, could there *be* a better setting for my allegory of Sin slain by the Lion of God?

— Except, says Peter, hands on hips, I'm jolly well alive, aren't I? Put that in your pipe and smoke it — I'm alive!

But as the golden dawn breaks, Blackstone only laughs, triumphant.

— Yes! And may the bells ring out the Lamb's resurrection!

• 3

And they do, scamps. Louder than all the bells of London, ringing out a Nazi's Christmas Day, they chime mad jubilation, and:

— Fuck! cries Flashjack. Look!

Atop the Stour the scruffs stands, the tick of a white rabbit's pocketwatch having marked Time Up and turned em to grim resolve, a quick flight on Erin's chariot in the ochenin, wolves left below to beseige them doors. At the peak of Blackstone's bastion's mighty pediment now, Foxtrot and Squirlet lashes ropes round waists for descent to that balcony Squirlet clocked, a sneaky entry point for their exfil mission. But:

— Look! says Flashjack.

They scarce hears him over the pandemonium of pealing, but the grabbings and pointings gets their peepers on target, to the south — oh, and the north now — to see, streaming in along the coast, a pincering attack of animal hordes. Bollocks! It's yer dreaming groanhuffs, scamps, so it is, *all* of em by the looks of it, and all gone mad, bleeding *rabid*. Proud lions, raging bulls, and bears with sore heads so befuddling, they's blind furious. All yer groanhuffs' snooty indignation's been unleashed and set upon em by them bells ringing out the glory of a Nazi's twisted righteousness.

Below, the leader of that wolf pack howls a command — more'n wild enough to cut through the cacophany — and the great pack splits, two charges driving off to meet the onslaught on each front. No time for faffing now, it's over the edge for scamp and scrag, Janie and Flashjack lowering em. But it's not just a ground assault, scamps. No, to north and south the skies are thick too with a mad menagerie of birds, great eagles and hawks and whatnot – gryphons too, by fuck! And on that pediment peak or dangling down the precipice, them scruffs is exposed.

Into battle then flies that sky chariot of Erin O'Morrigan, with that ginormous rook – surely the greatest Rake as ever dreamt – and all them carrion birds as *looks* malevolent but ain't half as nasty as the swans diving in at em, fucking velociraptors in an emperor's ermine, vicious as a rapist god. As the sort of god who'd wear an eagle's form to scrobble a kid – like them going for Foxy and Squirlet now. Lily's rifle fires – CRACK! – and fires CRACK! – but ropes is slashed. They's falling, falling...
  And snatched to safety by a rook's claws latching on their backs!

• 4

And with a swoopy spiral up, a glimpse! Picture it: Beast Blackstone on that balcony, lion head and eagle wings; Peter beside, aghast at the battle; Peter beside, a glint of shiv in hand.
  He jinks sharp to stomp on Blackstone's tootsies, spins to drive the shiv two-handed into Blackstone's thigh, yanks back, flips grip and drops, shiv spiking foot now. Hands under a heel jerked up; heave-ho, and that fucker's over the edge. Now, quick! He can't hardly think for that godawful clamouring gospel of salvation, white souls called to conquer nations, but Foxtrot's schooled him: focus!

Round the innards of that bell tower, he bounds, railing to rope to railing, not a thought for the drop to where's them minions works the bells. He slashes, slices, channeling all the savvy them scruffs could give, to find the weak spots that should – *yes!* And with a snaplashing *CRACKARACK-CRACKETY!* ropes flying all ways, bells go swinging like demolition balls to shatterings, splinterings. He barely makes it to the balcony as the whole thing falls. And barely dodges Blackstone hurtling back in with a beat of wings, a roar.
  And, oh. As Blackstone wheels... where can he go?

Just as that reverend bastard's tasting retribution though, what's this? A shadow of black wings upon our boy backed to the balcony's edge, a glance above. And Peter springs to balance, thumbs nose and springs again, arms reaching. Why, he's leapt to snatch two whatsits tumbling to him: wishsnuff and chanter, courtesy of one scamp, one scrag and one ginormous fucking raven. And Peter's dropped from sight, and Blackstone's bellowing, launching after him, but *whooooosh!* now, Peter rockets back, with chanter to his lips, to sneeze a roundhouse punch of wind what knocks that Nazi back into his hole – *KERSPLAT!*

It ain't the most melodious fluting ever, that's for sure, cause the shrillest tuneless walloper of a whistleblast were Peter's aim, and having popped that wishsnuff tin while's plummeting, got the peppery lot of it *whoomf* in his face, well, one almighty fucking sneeze give him his goal and then some. Why, from the spout of water down in that loch twixt Stour and sea, some whale as makes Moby Dick look minnowy is either black affronted or besmitten. But there's a beauty in just punching Nazis in the face, innit.
    – *Lamb,* sniffs Peter. *Kids* have horns too, you know.

• 5

So, scamps, the War on Nazi Christmas as Peter turns to see: on the ground below, them wolves and animal hordes smashing into each other, wave after wave; in the sky above, them rooks and avian adversaries a whirling of pinions and talons, the Morrigan in her chariot carving a path of slaughter, Foxtrot and Squirlet dropped with her now to mind her back with sword and shurikens; and between, on the cliff's edge, Lily as sniper, barrel propped on the rucksack, Janie and Flashjack fighting gryphons and hippogriffs, two streetfighting scruffs against yer noblest beasts of heraldry and myth.

To the west now, though, from down the gentler slope of that landslip ridge, from the distant treeline, beneath the clamour of battle, that scofflaw and scallywag hears a hum, a buzz, a whiny drone, getting louder, louder, *louder,* until, by fuck, a billow of black bursts from the pines, a roiling stormfront cloud of...
    – Fucking midges? says Flashjack. Oh, *fuck off.*
    But it is, scamps. Not just from Blackstone's bullies neither, no, but from every dreaming twerp in the world, every dick, prick, hick and outright Hitlerfuckinjugend; oh, it's every bigoty spite groanhuffs can cram into a brat's bonce.

– Right, says Flashjack. Fuck this shit.
    And he's off, leaping and sliding down the icy rock they's perched on, to land on one knee, right fist forward, glowing red hot, *white* hot, blasting a wave of heat to vapourise every patch and skimmering of snow in its path, to shrivel the heather and grass all the way down that slope, down, down,

until that parched gorse meets the oncoming storm of insect hate, until that billowing mass is flowing over it.

Closer... Closer... Now!

And Flashjack slaps his palm down on that carpet of kindling and it lights like petrol.

He's only bought em time though, scamps – a fire like that burns out quick as it's lit – so it's back to the others pronto. And if there's gryphon's noggins flying at each swish of Janie's swords, hippogriffs stiffed with Lily's every shot, they's caught in the path of a storm thickening to solid even as it rushes in. But wait:

– Janie, the Stamp! cries Lily with a leap and scramble to Flashjack's shoulder. Come on!

Cause it's Peter swooping down toward em, reaching hands for them, clasping, soaring up, away. Hooray!

– Other hand! says Peter to Flashjack. Hot, hot, hot!

• 6

– Brace yourselves, bairns! Erin's shouting elsewheres and meantimes. We're going down!

And Squirlet and Foxtrot clings to a side each of that sleek black beast of a sky-chariot, clutched in the claws of one giant rook doing its fuckmost to brake the descent, but still streaking down like a B-52 with its last engine kaput. Even with one final defiant fury of effort from that rook, the landing's a bone-rattling bounce and jounce then bone-shattering smash as sends em all headlong and tumbling, the world a whirling blur until they rolls to their broken ragdoll flops.

First gasped awake, eyes on the skies now, leg braced for a quick shove on the knee to force a crooked shinbone straight, Squirlet's doing her best to hurry along her mending, what with Foxtrot and Erin down and defenceless, when – *thank fuck!* – she clocks the others soaring in, not a fuckload more controlled in their landing, but at less speed, so's it's only a stumbly run for Janie and a dive roll for Flashjack when Peter can't hold em no more. In a tick they's at her side, getting orders barked at em.

– Foxy's arm, she says. Over there.

– You can fly, you can swim, she says to Peter and Lily. Think!

They just blinks at her – bloomin newbs. By the jerkety cracks of Foxy's and Erin's forms, they'll be sprung back soonish, and Squirlet's *mostways* functional now, but it's only one ginormous raven and one lollopy direwolf fallen back to help Flashjack and Janie defend the Stamp, t'others busy on two ground fronts and an aerial riot. Backs to the shore, they ain't scarpering nowheres. And pouring over the Stour's edge now like some volcano's black spew of ashcloud, comes spite made flesh.

Oh, but from elsewheres: salvation!

RATATATATA! It's two satyrs, Goggles and Tubbs, on motorbike and sidecar, with Polish centaurs galloping afters and a misfit hellion mob behind, all armed to the teeth and blasting berserker-mode, with machine-guns, rifles and pistols from the Home Guard armoury, all the firepower to be scavenged from dreams of cowboys and cops-and-robbers – why, there's even slingshots, catapults, longbows, crossbows. Them satyrs only broke that Blackstone's spell, innit – albeit inadvertently, argy-bargying so panicky over the Nazi boat they found docked in the harbour, one Upsadaisy Fagspuffer overhears and sings out:

– Blimey crikey! The game's a bogey!

• 7

RATATATATA! PTCHOW! PTCHOOM! Them scruffs hears the racket of attack, but with the thick of battle, they don't see nuffink, can't tell what's happening, till suddenly it's the Red Sea parting, animals leaping everyways, and smashing through the stramash comes that bike and the oddball battalion. But even as the southern front's taken, Blackstone's beasts crushed between wolves and hellions, to the north their allies is being overrun, the line collapsing, until it's hordes racing toward each other again, to crash in the middle.

And from the Stour above, the black cascade still crashes down, pouring onto the slopes now.

Down it comes, scamps, oh, the torrent of spites, surging down over the battle, swallering all in its path, friend and foe alike, poor wolves and hellions and centaurs driven mad by a thousand bites, but their adversaries no less prey to the feeding frenzy. And for every hellion whipping a gas mask to their face, there's another *choking* on the swarm. It's fucking *hoaching* with em midges, scamps, *hoaching*. Why, against this even Flashjack's hellfire heatblast won't be more'n flamethrower versus tsunami.

And worse, there's shapes forming in it, scamps. Writhings and slother, flurryings and snicketings.

– *Squirrrrrlet*, says Peter.

– We need out of here *now*, says Squirlet.

A flick of her wrist thunks a shuriken into a kangaroo's jugular, blood spurting. Flashjack's pistols downs a tiger, Janie's swords a bear. And rapier and spear flashes too now, Foxy and Erin back in action. But yer indescribable horror of a gazillion pests fused as an Addanc's flesh plows inexorably toward em over the battle.

– Ooh, wait! says Peter.

– I've an idea! says Lily.

They looks at each other in startlement.

– What were you thinking? says one.

– What were *you* thinking? says t'other.

– Just do it! snaps Squirlet. Both of you!

As Peter goes rocketing into the air, Lily springs too, bounding weavy through the fray for Erin O'Morrigan, eyes on that belt where Keen's horns hangs. But it's not the right horn she's going for, scamps, the one what heals all wounds. Oh, no, cause being a scamp, she'd asked that Rake bold as buttons, *What the fuckety?* (to all *intensive porpoises* leastways, as they says) with respect to one horn, and been told of both. So it's Keen's *left* horn she leaps to nab and scarper with, headed for the shore, for the waves crashing wild upon the rocks.

As Lily goes sploosh into the surf, Peter seems out to make a splash too – in yer opening night song and dance spectacular down at the London Palladium sorta way, cause for some reason unfathomable to his newfound crib-mates, this scrag's took it in his head to give a rousing solo hornpipe rendition of Glenn Miller's *In the Mood*. Which is laudably capricious, maybe's even apt to Flashjack's acrobatic combat style, but don't seem of much *practical* assistance in defeating a bloody great midge monster.

Unlike, say, the mighty hornblast as turns all heads to the kelpie cavalry charge.

• 8

Out of the waves they comes, like they was *born* of em, white beasts with kelp bestraggling manes and tails, great galloping warhorses binding the brawn of Clydesdales with the sleek grace of Arabians, a wave-born cavalry what vaults overhead to crash into the enemy *as* a wave, rearing up and whirling, turning black with midges stuck to flesh, and galloping back to the water, the next wave vaulting over their heads for *their* assault.

And out to sea, one great white nightmare rears, an otter astraddle flicking seaweed reins and whooping a warcry what's sorta... Comanche meets ceilidh.

Thundering in on her steed comes Lily now, even swinging down on one seaweed stirrup – I shit you not, scamps – to bounce back up with rifle and cowboy hat snatched in her paws. And there's a steed for each of her compadres galloping tight behind her, slowing no more'n enough for them to grab reins and leap to mounted.

Oh, but even as they does, they sees: that Addanc, it's adapting, writhings splitting off between the kelpies, slothers skittering to reform out among the battling packs. Flurrying skitterings fuses into figures almost human... in a demonic droid skeleton sorta way.

So it's time to offsky, scamps. Retreat, regroup, rethink how's the fuck to nobble this Addanc, cause they ain't getting past it to Blackstone, and they *cannot* fucking lose the Stamp. On top of, y'know, accidentally dooming the one place innumerable scruffs ever felt safe.

Over the water they gallops then, veering south after Erin's lead – for the Sound of Raaarrrsay, she calls back, Loch Inert, the mouth of the Auld'n'Loopy. It'll mean a wee stretch overland, but with rivers and lochs along the valley, they'll can cut through to Loch Slappy. Grotternish's lost, but while Dun Straich still... still...

– Whateffer is that laddie up to? Erin exclaims.

Cause through all's this palaver of a cavalry charge and daring rescue, why, flying high in the sky, Peter he's been tootling every tune he knows from *We'll Meet Again* to *Over the Rainbow*, and as he kicks into *Auld Lang Syne* now, off to their right... a great geyser erupts, from them lochs between Stour and sea it must be.

– He's neffer...

And she veers her steed to a sharp clockwise turn around Ham Isle, turning west, northwest, back toward the Stour.

– A shanty, laddie! she cries. Give her a shanty!

• 9

Whatever might she mean, scamps? What might that Rake be minding of a chanter's power so's she'd click to that scrag's brainwave? What might's Peter be figgering his fife could tootle to their aid if only he can chance on the dance it can't resist, suss out the strain, the right refrain?

I'll tell yer what it *ain't*, scamps. Whatever he's mad-fancied to whistle up with the Silver Chanter, it ain't what rises now – not at Peter's piping, but at Blackstone's bellow from his balcony, at canting spittly fanatical as Adolf's ranted from that eyrie beneath the pediment's peak.

It ain't the Old Man Peter's playing for, but it's the Old Man as shudders now, and them nearby juts of rock poking up around, a ring of em sorta, near half a dozen. They judders, then jolts – *CRACKOOSH!* – and, fuck me, the whole bleeding circle of em pushes ten feet upwards from beneath the earth, clods of muck and gorse 'sploding up and showering down like's a grenade went off. And KERCKOOOOOM! another thrust, except this one brings a *pillar* of stone bursting from below, shooting up into the sky, earth raining down as from yer bleeding *doodlebug's* detonation.

Up and up it shoots, high as that pediment, *higher*, past Blackstone's hand raised in an upturned claw and echoing it, scamps, this pillar what dwarfs the Old Man as an arm does a thumb – because that's what it bleeding well *is*. It's the fricking left arm of that sleeping giant what has the Old Man for its thumb. And as Blackstone's hand flattens and turns from palm-in to palm-out, as his arm lowers its angle from straight up to the fucking forty-five degrees of some fucking southpaw Nazi salute, so too does that sleeping giant's, mate.

Now Blackstone's other hand thrusts up in a fist, and another pillar explodes from the earth, its base like's the first's on that great looming ridge of the Stour as now looks, with Blackstone sweeping his arms outward, like nuffink less than the shoulders of some grey stone titan hung on a cross or hoisted as puppet, that pedimenty outcrop its bonce dangling limp.

Not limp for long though, scamps, cause as Blackstone sweeps his arms down, the giant copies him in yer most gobsmacking game of *Simon Says* ever. And as Blackstone pushes down, the giant pushes itself up.

• 10

Oh, scamps, is it Fingumy Cool himself, who built the Giant's Causeway as stepping stones from Ireland to Scotland? Or that bigger bastard Beenandunnit, what Fingumy had to overcome? Or even Bawler, King of them Fumers, brawnier still, who'd his eye smashed right out the back of his bonce by a stone from Lookit's sling? No, scamps, this fucker's bigger and older'n *all* of em combined, goes back so far, why, some says he'd to use Noah's Ark as float to survive the bloomin Flood.

The mighty Gog his grampa, McGog his pappy, it's Og Mac McGog, scamps, Og himself.

Hal Duncan

***

Fixed back in yer days of the Tower of Babble, tweaked to the biggest bastard ever strode the Earth, first of all hellions to say *fuck this for a game of sodjies* and escape after Keen and Able to the Land of Nod, settled down on yer isle of Skye for a nice wee kip and been asleep there ever since, dreaming so deep he's even asleep in his dreams... It's Og. And he's still asleep, scamps. Even as he hauls himself up out of the ground to tower over the chasm what was his bed, this ain't no awakening.

No, cause as that great outcrop rises to reveal itself as, yes, his behatted bonce, as Og's face comes clear now, Peter in the air above Loch Leathering and even them scruffs astraddle their kelpies in the sea beyond him, they can see the eyes in it are shut. So what's steering this Gargantua in his slumber? As that mighty head turns its blank gaze from the chaos of critters fleeing below upon Peter and the others, what sense is turning it as if to see?

As in some mystical lore of Lily's mum's land, scamps, it's a *third* eye.

An hole bored smack dab in the centre of his forehead, a bulge of panelled glass built as some bulbous porthole, why, it's like nuffink so much as the nose blister of a Boeing B-17 Flying Fortress, with Blackstone inside it where's the bombardier would sit; but it's the *pilot* he is, scamps, and this his cockpit, and he ain't sat in it but suspended, held aloft by the invisible writhings and slother of the Addanc, every move he makes Simon-Saysed into the sleeping giant's limbs by that puppeteering executioner of its master's egomaniacal will.

Correctomundo, scamps.

Fuck.

Part Eight

• 1

Aloft in the air like Blackstone, but held there by a power of whimsy and fanciful high-jinks, (as opposed to yer parasitic puppeteering monster-from-the-deep fuelled by delusion and in thrall to fascist zeal, like,) Peter's so dumbstruck at the sight of this thing, why, if his jaw weren't attached he'd has to come to his senses and dive like the crackers to catch it before it splashed into Loch Leathering below him and were lost forever. Not a peep comes from his pipe as he hovers there gawping... until he hears the voice crying out below.

– A shanty, laddie! booms Erin O'Morrigan.

Charging ashore at Beery Bay – straight in the path of that giant if he strides out seaward to stomp em, scamps – charging over the beach and up grassy slopes, to rear her steed upon a mound at the head of Loch Leathering, the others hot at her heels – or her kelpie's hooves, rather – she calls up at him with all the two-fisted thigh-slapping gusto of a goddess of war too lusty for life to keep the job.

– By yer prickety horns, my clever lad! she booms. It's a *shanty* she'll be after!

But of course! Oh, how could he be so daft not to see it, scamps? Here he is with a chanter as might as well be a bleeding hornpipe in his hands, and it's that great spout of water what answered his whistleblast facepunching of Blackstone as the light bulb above his noggin went off over. It's what he suddenly savvied must lie sunken and snoozy under the loch's calm waters

– it's only *that* he's been trying to raise all this time and never once thought to rouse it with a shanty!

– Oh, I'm the perfect featherbrained chump, says he.

And with a twirl, he dives, pipe to lips, bursting out with a *toot tootle-oot, tootle-oot toot-root-toot* what gets a *whoohoo!* from Flashjack, on account of him reputedly being the very drunken sailor that ditty's about, with all them verses what says to chuck him in the longboat, or turn a hosepipe on him, or whatever,' aktcherly savvy advice on dealing with a scallywag liable to spark powderkegs while's sober. Gets a geyser what near hosepipes Peter too, scamps, and a mightier steamboaty *WHOOHOOOO!* with it.

And hey ho, up she rises: the Good Ship Whimsy.

• 2

Oh, how can I conjure it for yer, scamps? Like yer sailing ships of old, sleek as a clipper, but grand as a galleon, and the oddest of any such vessel yer ever did see, for in place of a mast it had a blooming tree trunk – *literally* blooming, cause blimey, even as its rigging breaks the loch's surface, all the buds of spring starts opening to minty green shoots; as the water streams from gunwales, half of em's darkening to summer's emerald; and as its bows carves its wake, why, there's the brightest ambery leaves of any autumn too.

A ship of all seasons is the Good Ship Whimsy, in blossom here but fruiting there, great juicy-looking globes of all colours, like oranges and peaches and plums ballooned up big as a bonce, as a beachball, bigger even, and maybe's *actual* balloons, cause that ship don't just rise out of the depths, but *out of the water* now. Or maybe's it's the great big whirlymajig atop it, with bibbons like helicopter blades reaching out an hundred and three feet wide, ribbons looped and twisted betwixt em as if to catch the wind, spin them bibbons like windmill sails.

Oh, it's the cunningest queer caprice of a ship, scamps, cause that whirlymajig's built not just to funnel the wind down for yer helicopter's lift, but to wangle and quangle it through the branches into knotholes all up and down that tree's hollow trunk. And all round the ship's hull, that tree's flutey roots pops out like cannons or exhausts. Why, it's a giant pipe organ in its innards, with valves what sends the air to port or starboard, fore or aft, to blast out in great contrabassoony didgeridooy *PHWOOOOOPS!* what'll jet it forward, veer it this way and that.

But that whirlymajig ain't whirly enough, it seems. She's afloat, she is, the Good Ship Whimsy, but no more'n a nipper's noggin above the water's surface, that elaborate Sunday hat of an external contraption engine spinning lazy as an hungover scofflaw, herself spluttering water from them exhausts but without the oomph to truly clear her pipes, poor thing. She tries, oh, she tries, with all the heart Peter toots into his choruses, but she ain't that young whippersnap Flashjack with a stripling's stamina to just belt it out.

    – Whistle up a wind, laddie! comes the cry. Whistle up a wind!

• 3

So the *up*-side of the hurricane Peter pipes from his perch on the bowsprit of the Good Ship Whimsy is its billows and blasts is most effective in battering back an army of midge myrmidons and a stone giant out to stomp that ship back into the depths it came from. The *down*-side is while's he's well over nine on yer Beaufort Wind Force Scale, aktcherly controlling the direction beyond *round and round* is another matter.

    – It's awfully good for a beginner, Lily calls up supportively.

    Which don't change the fact the ship's in the hurricane's eye, becalmed.

– Och, she's no catching it, bairns! cries Erin. We'll have to hoik her to the winds. You two, wait here. You two, with me.

    In a tick, with a leap and a swing, she's hustling up a rope and aboard, Flashjack and Janie right behind. And it's: *into the tree, monkeys; to port, laddie; you to starboard; lash these tight*. And in a tock, there's ropes being tossed below, to Foxtrot and Squirlet – *catch and latch em!* – and a holler to Lily on the kelpie queen to lead the charge.

    – Now hi-ho and heave, cries Erin. Ride, bairns, RIDE!

And, oh now, picture it! Thundering hell for leather down Loch Leathering, galloping straight fucking at yer, this wild trio of kelpies with a pirate spurring this one, ninja flicking reins on that one, and one rootin-tootin cowboy otter out in front whooping. Picture it! Hooves pounding water to spray, kicking clouds of it behind, clouds out of which she rises, like the biggest and best kite in the world, the Good Ship Whimsy, rising higher, scamps, higher, her whirlymajig catching the wind now, wangling it, quangling it down into her pipes and out to a mighty steamboat *PWHOOOOORRRRRRP!*

It's a mad scramble then for Foxtrot and Squirlet up their ropes, a *Hang on, what about me?* for Lily, and a bold leap down for Erin to land astraddle behind the otter as Lily's steed slows from gallop to canter to trot, snorts great salty spumes from its nostrils, harrumphy as rider.

– Well, I never! says Lily.

– Och, yer needed down here, lass, says the Rake. It's ye and me now, together.

And a clap on the shoulder fills Lily's heart.

– And ye've made an auld dear's century, sonsy lass, Erin winks. I've always fancied to ride Keen's kelpies.

• 4

And as Lily, with the Morrigan herself riding pillion, rears her steed for another blast of Keen's horn, to call the cavalry of the sea – *To me!* – in the skies above, the Good Ship Whimsy bellows what seems a halloo but's aktcherly a singalong with her pilot. That wheel on her quarterdeck aft of the mast? Ain't but a decorative fancy, it seems, when Foxtrot's spin does nuffink. No, it's Peter's hornpipe helms her in call and response of them exhausts – as *is* cannons too, Flashjack finds with a giant peach scrumped, fumbled butterfingers down an hole, and FfffPWOOOP!

– Ooooooooooooooooh!

So it's Squirlet in the crow's nest treehouse perched high in a fore-branch's fork – trust her to spy that hidey pronto and nab it, eh? – calling shots back to her powder monkeys, Flashjack and Janie, aswing on vines, scrambling rope ladders, plank bridges, plucking them humongous fruits to lob em like basketballs, roll em down branches, into this huge knothole, that woodpecker's nest. And it's Foxtrot discovering the use of that wheel, spinning three o'clock, nine o'clock, fire away!

And it's Peter afore fluting *Speed, Bonnie Boat*, steering into the whirlwind – and fireworks now, scamps, 'sploding starboard and port.

And fuck yer Pickaninny Indians of a groanhuff's half-arsery, it's Tiger Lily Furiosa, with her kelpie-mounted tribe of queer freak hellions charging them boys what's lost in straight white spite, charging Blackstone's Addanc-driven skeletal droid minions made of umptillion midges each, storming the ack-ack batteries they's sandbagged up the slopes. It's her and Erin pointing squads of wolves and ravens this way, that way, into the breach, scruffs' bestest friends, and crack that wall of insect black! It's Lily's Lancers smacking thwack through corpses in the Addanc's grip now too, dumb groanhuffs' bonkers bestial dreams. Attack!

And the starboard guns of the Good Ship Whimsy blast a broadside fusillade, pounding the giant's bonce with conkers big as cannonballs and twice as hard, every one of em solid as a seasoner baked, boiled in vinegar, and varnished by the sneakiest cheat. The Whimsy's pipe organ peashooters blasts, but oh, though they rattles that bonce, they miss the blister, and up comes one hand to defend, another to swipe – a near miss, whew! But as Blackstone opens his lion's gob to roar, the giant's jaw drops too.

And out they streams, pale riders, bloodcurdling... Nazi elves on alicorns.

• 5

It's only bleeding unicorn pegasuses, scamps, innit! Unicorn bleeding pegasuses as the steeds of yer high and haughty latter-day Teutonic Templars of the Order of Saint Mithras. And oh, by fuck, if piping Peter in the Land of Nod might be the inspiration for Edwardian fancy or Athenian myth, these fuckers flying in with Mausers rattling might be the veritable bad seed rooted in dreams and sprouted to all history's fuckery in the name of nobilitude and purity, from Roman legions, through kiddy-scrobbling crusaders, to Ripper Vicky's waiftakers with their statues in the Stamp's vault in the Institute.

Flighty Peter can dart up from the bullets aimed at bowsprit. Squirlet can duck into her treehouse for shelter from the strafing. Flashjack and Janie can bounce and swing to dodge through the thrash of machine-gunned foliage with all the agility of yer harlequin Scarlequin and a Longpins with a spider monkey's tail. But Foxtrot can only dive from the wheel on the quarterdeck, defenseless. But wait!

– To starboard, shouts Squirlet. Flashjack, on your two!

And he looks, he sees, fuck me, glory be, then he's sprinting down a branch to jump and swing feet-first: *Down the hatch!*

And *KAPHWOOOOOOOOP!* It's a cannon's boom and a steamboat's toot rolled into one, and Flashjack fired as a human cannonball, wheel spun to two o'clock just in time by a Foxtrot what pays a bloody price for it, battered by bullets in his back, and down. Oh noes!

But it's Flashjack roaring up into the sky now, oh, astraddle a gorgeous beastie of blue underbelly and green back, as heard them bells what sent yer other beasties mad, and didn't like em one little bit, come soaring, now roaring, spitting furious to see *Nazi knights.*

It's Spitfire, scamps. That's right!

Whooshing to the defence of the Good Ship Whimsy they comes, the dragon spitting fireballs fast as any Mauser, Flashjack with his highwayman's flintlock – what fortuitously ain't the one shot wonder and *Fuckety fuckety!* fumbling to reload as yer *actual* pistols of that era was, yer Land of Nod being graciously liberal with its ammo and lax with its practicalities, as yer might expect, I s'pose, of summat built in accordance with nippers' dreams.

Why, any more fast and loose with its How Shit Works, and it might give yer Hollywood movies a run for their money, truth be told.

• 6

If Flashjack's gun has an 'andily inexhaustible supply of shots though, not-so-fortuitously them Mausers does too, and these ain't yer Hollywood movie Nazis as couldn't hit the back of a bus speeding away from em down a straight road over a bridge yer groanhuff make-believer wants to go boom with all them pursuing Nazis on it. No, scamps, it's only the sheer bloody aerial acrobatics of Spitfire as keeps the bullets thwacking into our scallywag to a *manageable* minimum, Spitfire looping the loop to blast an alicorn from the sky in great hurtling chunks of burning flesh.

But down on the hills them meteors of flaming alicorn meat hits like fucking mortar shells, a kelpie queen is down, and if an otter might ride a great lolloping whelp of a wolf, a Rake can't but stand atop a pile of dead stags, spear twirling and stabbing, fighting her fiercest to fend off writhings and slother she can't see, blast it, except where's the dragonfire splatters and sticks, them great burning gobbers of gelatinous jet fuel saliva Spitfire swoops down to rattle at the Addanc, as he tries to draw them Nazis on alicorns away from the Whimsy.

With a blast of his flintlock, Flashjack puts a shot between an elf's eyes. With a squeeze of knees, he brings Spitfire up from a raking round the giant's feet – what shows a glimpse of the vast horror of the Addanc wrappling it – to torch the last alicorn worrying the Whimsy, and – hang on! – bank hard, dive again.

Ain't often that scallywag has a bright idea, mate, but when he do it's fucking *incendiary*. So now, he weaves a wide pendulous zigzag of strafing to see where dragonfire just splatters hillside, where it swirls *above* it, thrashing.

– North, he cries.

And Lily and Erin's in a tightening ring of puppet creature death, the Whimsy's headed ramming speed, guns blazing, for a giant's bonce, but with a hand snatching up to crush em, even as Flashjack, alicorn Nazis on his tail, races north, sleek Spitfire's fireballs tracing writhe and slother to its roots –

of course! – in Loch Shianta – *fucking duh!*

And it's *dive, boy, dive!* a hail of dragonfire pounding, searing, slicing the Addanc's rotten heart clean from its vast unspeakable mass of flurrying and snicketing appendages, to slice the puppeteer's strings.

And every corpse its grip were dancing simply drops.

• 7

And even as limbs and corpses rains down on the battlefield round Lily and Erin, as them skeletal droid minions all just whoomfs back to clouds of midges, aimless gnats smirred on the wind... high above, a glass blister smashes at a bowsprit's impact. As Blackstone drops, the Addanc's latchings severed from his will, that bowsprit nearly spears the fucker. Oh, but no. His raised hand's echoed in stone what's snatched the Good Ship Whimsy in its grasp at the last squirmy latchings of an Addanc's final act.

And out he comes, on eagle wings extending, roaring for Scruffian blood.

– To Peter! cries Foxtrot sprinting down the deck.

And even as his pirate rapier's lobbed like ninja's dagger, Squirlet's swashbuckling a rope from crow's nest down to snatch it, winding round the treetrunk like a maypole, launching it onward.

– To Peter! she cries.

And Janie's monkey-swinging branch to branch, leaping to nab that sword, darting nimble with her tail for balance to a branch's bouncing tip, to hurl it on. And in that spittly speech she really oughtn't be so shy about – she really oughtn't – why, in that very moment, she give Peter his Scruffian name.

– Peacher! she cries.

It's not just some easy nab and jab though, scamps, not with that bastard flying out, hands clamping Peter's throat: *I'll wring your neck, filthy scruff!* Peter has to think sharp, kick the fucker in his bollocks, but that just makes him tighten his grip, start twisting with the throttling like's to tear his noggin right fucking off. But, aha! Of course! And Peter stamps a tackety boot, hard as fuck, right into that wound he left in Blackstone's thigh, where's he were going for the femural artery. And *now* the fucker lets go, Peter kicks himself free and –

– Peacher!

Peter pirouettes to see the rapier soaring, backflips, catches, loops and stabs – straight in the heart, scamps! He skewers that lionheaded, eagle-winged cuntfucker straight through his rotten Nazi heart!

But Blackstone's hand shoots out, scamps, snatches his throat again. Oh, the bastard's mortal wounded, but he ain't gone yet, and it's a death grip squeezing now, and the dying lion's jaws are opening wide, scamps, angling – oh, fuckety fuck – to chomp Peter's Stamp right off his chest, closing in...

CRACK!

And it's a bullet in the brain from a Springfield Trapdoor – hallefuckinlujah! – crackshot Lily from gobsmackerty hundred feet below.

• 8

It's victory, scamps, victory! And take that for yer fucking Merry Nazi Christmas! The Land of Somewhere Safe is saved – huzzah! – and safe again for every scruff – well, okay, not *entirely* safe when's Peter's celebratory tootling wakes the giant Og himself to an earthshaking jig as sends them allies scarpering from splatterisings, Foxtrot shouting: *A lullaby! A lullaby!* But then ain't nowhere's never *entirely* safe, eh, scamps? We just makes it safe as we can, just fights to *make* it safe for ourselves and others, and the less safe it is, the fiercer we fights.

Eh, Slickspit, ain't that right?

So it's a week-long ceilidh in Dun Tarakin's streets, scamps, with Polish centaurs prancing like foals, and satyrs gamboling like kids, jumping up on anything what's higher than their noggins as goats is wont to do. Right through to Hogmanay it goes, with aerial acrobatics and fireworks from Spitfire as it turns a New Year what Erin says, as they feasts in Dun Straich, time being bonkers here, could well be *next* New Year, or somewhen afters, *could* be whichever New Year will see the war's end... if that's what they wants – for the safety of the Stamp, like.

So maybe's it ain't a War Meeting them scruffs has, strictly speaking, them talking peace, but then again... If they can take the Stamp back to a waking world safe from Nazis now, well, all em orphan strays out there, all em Scruffians-to-be... Ain't making things safe as we can for *them* the war still to be won?

That's why they decides it's hometime – most of em anyways.

– I think I should like to stay a *little* while longer? says Lily to Erin.

– And oughtn't *someone* go looking for Keen and Able? says Peter. On a ship, perhaps?

Oh, the adventures them two had! Yer might even have heard a peep of em via one groanhuff's half-arsed fancification of a half-remembered dream. Of course, that bungling don't explificate what it were *made* all Peacher Peckerpipe's boys feel sorta lost and want to play with *just boys, ta*, nor how Sniperlily Tuckerinny's tribe of wildlings was all them *others*, girls and boys and elsewises, as found Peter's gay bratchelor fraternity *a bit tame, to be honest*. And fuck that pile of pish about mothers and thimbles, and that racist monicker on Lily's tribe, fuck's sake...

Sorry.

Anyway...

• 9

So Peter tootles the Good Ship Whimsy to anchor over Dun Straich, to keep any magical malarkey within that castle's sphere of containment, and they runs the Faerie Flag up as its colours. They has to damn near prise Flashjack away from a tearful farewell to Spitfire where's he's latched around the dragon's neck, and if it weren't for the fact the Stamp *has* to travel by scofflaw courier with an hellion escort, and Foxtrot reminding him he *can* visit any time he dreams, well, that scallywag might have never left. But finally, *finally*, they gets him up the rope.

It's up to the quarterdeck then for Erin, a wee pinch of wishsnuff, a sneeze, but instead of some rocketing flight off into the wild blue yonder, she just sets to turning the wheel in the queerest manner, clockwise and widdershins, widdershins and clockwise, roundabout mostways, a jigger back – why, it's like nuffink so much as Vermintrude Toerag cracking a combination safe.

– Give us *We'll Meet Again*, laddie, she says then to Peter.

And with fond farewells all round, she huchles those Brawling Bastables to that treetrunk's base, a great gaping knothole, and in she sends em, one by one.

One by one they hops in, and in a tick they's hooshing down and round, whooshing helter skelter as on some waterpark flume, scamps, only with a force ten gale instead of water, blasting em faster, faster, round and around, and up, firing up and out – *wahey! oh, deary me! fuuuuuck – ! aaaaaaaah!* – Flashjack's acrobatic (and even dramatic) landing on one knee somewhat spoiled by them others, one by one, landing atop him, them all ending up in a guddly heap just a little away from the hollow trunk of the Elfin Oak in Kensington Gardens what they'd been squooffed from.

They couldn't hardly believe it when they comes out of Hyde Park by Wellington Arch, finds themselves toddling up to a Piccadilly Circus jumping with news of Victory in Europe, packed with partying Londoners and lit to high heavens – bleeding searchlights and all. As Zoe Gail herself stands on a balcony in her top hat and tails singing *I'm Going to Get Lit Up When the Lights Go Up in London*, why, it were only the sight of a scrag lifting a drunk's leather and legging it...

Only then did they truly *know* they was back home, safe and sound.

• 10

Snug in Quip's ensconcing cuddle, nooked between the scallywag's knees and wrappled in a way that couldn't be further from an Addanc's thrall, Slickspit Hamshankery, prentice fabbler, watches Gob lean back with the fabble's end, stretch and crick his neck. The rapt hush – until now, that is – of the gaggle of scamps in a horseshoe around him... that might well have a wee echo of the Addanc's thrall to it, right enough, given the way it whoomfs to a cloud of chattery babble and fidgeting now as Gob clambers to his feet.

– Right, says he. Shust and snatch some kip.

Like an ear-skritched mutt, Slick angles his head into the strokes of thumb where Quip's right hand idles in the crook of neck and shoulder, the left rested over his heart, arm tucked round under his own, and with the two of them dug down into the sleeping bag to boot, he could almost doze off himself. What with Gob's penchant for piss breaks and pauses to skin up, suspiciously synched with dramatic twists – *look, me throat's just sore, Gob's truth* – it must be nearing dawn now. In other circumstances, it'd be a wonder the scamps aren't asleep already.

As the nippers bumshuffle, inchworm and elbow, in their bundlings of sleeping bags and blankies, into a *right moger*, as Gob would put it, of squidge and sprawl halfway between a pile of pups and a bin bag of togs half-inched from an Oxfam's doorway and dumped by a scallywag on the crib floor, the fabbler tips Slick and Quip a nod c'mere. Neither's exactly hop-to-it peachy keen in unhuddling from their cosy nest, but with a lazy limbering and a flapple of sleeping bag round shoulders, they join Gob as he peels bin bag from window.

– Should get ready to offsky soon, says Gob.

Outside, shadow is still all you can really make out, but there's form to it now, if you look upwards, a scraggly thick scribble of branches and twig, splotched with crow's nests and, after a night of rain to clear the sky, silhouetted against the deep blue of twilight's twin. The ochenin. In the dark, they can hide. In the light, they'll fight. In between, in this dead time before dawn, it's safe to move. Safe to retreat, regroup, rethink. Well, not *entirely* safe. Never *entirely* safe.

But safe enough for now.

About the Author

Hal Duncan is the author of the novels *Vellum* and *Ink*, more recently *Testament*, and an ongoing series of Scruffians chapbooks, along with numerous short stories, poems, essays, even some musicals. Homophobic hatemail once dubbed him "THE.... Sodomite Hal Duncan!!" (sic), and you can find him online at http://www.halduncan.com or at his Patreon for readings, revelling in that role.

Cover art by Ben Baldwin

NewCon Press Novella Set 4: Strange Tales

Gary Gibson – Ghost Frequencies

Susan MacDonald knows she's close to perfecting a revolutionary new form of instantaneous communication, but unless she makes a breakthrough soon her project will be shut down. Do the odd sounds – snatches of random conversation and even music – that are hampering her experiments represent the presence of 'ghosts' as some claim, deliberate sabotage as suggested by others, or is there a more sinister explanation?

Adam Roberts – The Lake Boy

Cynthia lives in a lakeside parish in Cumbria, where none suspect her blemished past. Then a ghostly scar-faced boy starts to appear to her and strange lights manifest over Blaswater. What of the astromomer Mr Sales, who comes to study the lights but disappears, presumed drowned, only to be found wandering naked days later with a fanciful tale of being 'hopped' into the sky and held within a brass-walled room? What of married mother of two Eliza, who sets Cynthia's heart so aflutter?

Ricardo Pinto – Matryoshka

Lost in Venice in the aftermath of the war, Cherenkov just wants to put his head down somewhere and sleep, but her copper hair snares his eye. She leads him to Eborius, a baroque land lost in time, and takes him on a pilgrimage across Sargasso seas in search of the Old Man, who dwells on an island where time follows its own rules. Last of his kind, the Old Man is the only being alive who may hold the answers Cherenkov craves.

Learning How to Drown
Cat Hellisen

Cat Hellisen is a South African writer of dark fantasy. She has the ability to conjure a sense of 'otherness' that most writers can only envy, casting grounded characters driven by passions and ambitions we can all recognise in situations that take a step away from the reality we know. Her stories have already featured in such venues as *Fantasy & Science Fiction* and *Tor.com*, and she is the winner of the Short Story Day Africa Prize.

Learning How to Drown represents Cat's best work to date, gathering together seventeen fabulous stories, two of which appear for the first time and all of which showcase why Cat Hellisen is being tipped as one to watch.

"Cat Hellisen is one of the most accomplished writers of African SFF. This fine collection gathers the best so far of her wondrous fictions."
— *Geoff Ryman, author of The Child Garden*

"Cat Hellisen is a writer of wonderful and allusive stories; rich, engaging and often unsettling. Be prepared to be both submersed – and transformed – by the gripping magic within!"
— *Nick Wood, author of Azanian Bridges*

"I loved this stunning collection of stories, every tale limned with beauty and steeped in a darkling strangeness that is absolutely unique. The bookshelves of any reader interested in the modern short story should proudly display a copy of Learning How To Drown front and centre."
— *Neil Williamson, author of The Moon King*

Learning How to Drown is available now as a paperback and as a numbered limited edition hardback, signed by the author.

IMMANION PRESS
Purveyors of Speculative Fiction

Songs to Earth and Sky – A Wraeththu Mythos Anthology by Storm Constantine & others

Six writers explore the eight seasonal festivals of the year, dreaming up new beliefs and customs, new myths, new dehara – the gods of Wraeththu. As different communities develop among Wraeththu, so fresh legends spring up – or else ghosts from the inception of their kind come back to haunt them. From the silent, snow-heavy forests of Megalithican mountains, through the lush summer fields of Alba Sulh, into the hot, shimmering continent of Olathe, this book explores the Wheel of the Year, bringing its powerful spirits and landscapes to vivid life. Nine new tales, including a novella, a novelette and a short story from Storm herself, and stories from *Wendy Darling, Nerine Dorman, Suzanne Gabriel, Fiona Lane* and *E. S. Wynn*. ISBN 978-1-907737-84-8 £11.99 $15.50 pbk

Venus Burning: Realms by Tanith Lee

Tanith Lee wrote 15 stories for the acclaimed US genre magazine 'Realms of Fantasy'. This book collects these stories for the first time, some of which only ever appeared in the magazine and will therefore be new to some of Tanith's fans. The stories in this collection are among her best work, in which Tanith takes myth and fairy tale tropes and turns them on their heads. Lush and lyrical, deep and literary, Tanith Lee created fresh poignant tales from familiar archetypes. This book also includes three previously uncollected stories from her Flat Earth mythos. ISBN 978-1-907737-88-6 £11.99, $17.50 pbk

Dark in the Day, Ed. by Storm Constantine & Paul Houghton

In the blink of an eye, around the corner, The Weird is everywhere, lurking beyond the margins of the mundane, emerging to dismantle our assumptions of reality. This collection celebrates evocative tales of oddness that span the genres of magic realism, the supernatural, the fantastical and the speculative. *Contributors include: Martina Bellovičová, J. E. Bryant, Glynis Charlton, Storm Constantine, Louise Coquio, Elizabeth Counihan, Krishan Coupland, Elizabeth Davidson, Siân Davies, Paul Finch, Rosie Garland, Rhys Hughes, Kerry Fender, Andrew Hook, Paul Houghton, Tanith Lee, Tim Pratt, Nicholas Royle, Michael Marshall Smith, Paula Wakefield, Ian Whates and Liz Williams.* ISBN: 978-1-907737-74-9 £11.99, $18.99 pbk

Salty Kiss Island by Rhys Hughes

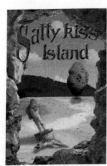

What is a fantastical love story? It isn't quite the same as an ordinary love story. The events that take place are stranger, more extreme, full of the passion of originality, invention and magic, as well as an intensification of emotional love. The stories in *Salty Kiss Island* are set in this world and others, spanning the spectrum of possible and impossible experiences, the uncharted territories of yearning, the depths and shoals of the heart, mind and soul. A love of language runs through them, parallel to the love that motivates their characters to feats of preposterous heroism, luminous lunacy and grandiose gesture. They include tales of minstrels and their catastrophic serenades, dreamers sinking into sequences of ever-deeper dreams, goddesses and mermaids, sailors and devils, messages in bottles that can think and speak but never be read, shadows with an independent life and voyagers of distant galaxies who are already at their destinations before they arrive.
ISBN: 978-1-907737-77-0, £11.99, $15.50 pbk

For more information on our titles visit
www.immanion-press.com